"If we're going to fight, why don't we make it permanent?"

"Leave the girl alone," Slocum said.

The gunman looked over at Slocum. "What did you say?"

"I said leave the girl alone."

"What the hell, mister? You think you're giving orders here?" the train robber asked. "I'm the one giving the orders here. And while we're at it, just put all your money in this hat."

"I've got a better idea," Slocum said. "You put the hat down and leave the car. If you do that, I'll let you live."

"You'll let *me* live? Are you crazy?"

"Do what I said, or die," Slocum said, calmly.

Suddenly the train robber sensed that Slocum meant business, and he pulled the hammer back on his pistol. That was as far as he got before Slocum pulled the trigger on his own gun, which he was holding under his hat. He blew a hole in his hat, but more importantly, opened up a hole in the robber's chest. Dropping his gun, the robber clutched his chest, and staggered back a few steps.

JAKE LOGAN

SLOCUM
AND THE WIDOW MAKER

JOVE BOOKS, NEW YORK

This is a work of fiction. Names, characters, places, and incidents either are the product of the author's imagination or are used fictitiously, and any resemblance to actual persons, living or dead, business establishments, events, or locales is entirely coincidental.

SLOCUM AND THE WIDOW MAKER

A Jove Book / published by arrangement with
the author

PRINTING HISTORY
Jove edition / July 2002

Copyright © 2002 by Penguin Putnam Inc.

All rights reserved.
This book, or parts thereof, may not be reproduced in any form
without permission.
For information address: The Berkley Publishing Group,
a division of Penguin Putnam Inc.,
375 Hudson Street, New York, New York 10014.

Visit our website at
www.penguinputnam.com

ISBN: 0-515-13336-1

A JOVE BOOK®
Jove Books are published by The Berkley Publishing Group,
a division of Penguin Putnam Inc.,
375 Hudson Street, New York, New York 10014.
JOVE and the "J" design
are trademarks belonging to Penguin Putnam Inc.

PRINTED IN THE UNITED STATES OF AMERICA

10 9 8 7 6 5 4 3 2 1

1

John Slocum dropped his saddle with a sigh of relief. Before him, bare railroad tracks stretched out across the bleak landscape, twin ribbons of iron touching the distant and empty horizons east and west. For the moment the tracks were no more comforting than the barren sand, rocks, and cactus of the desert itself. But finding them was John's salvation, for he knew a westbound train would be passing this way sometime before sundown.

His Appaloosa had stepped in an unseen gopher hole just after dawn this morning. With the horse's leg broken in two places, Slocum had no choice but to put the poor creature down. It had not been an easy task, carrying a saddle more than ten miles on his shoulder, but he knew the railroad was near and he didn't want to lose his saddle. Besides, it made a pretty good pillow, and that was precisely the use Slocum put it to as he lay down alongside the track to await the train.

Thirty miles west of John's present position was the town of Prosperity. Despite its optimistic name, Prosperity was little more than a flyblown speck on the wide-open range.

It had reached its peak when it was End of Track, a "hell on wheels," with enough cafés, saloons, and bawdy houses to take care of the men who were building the railroad. But as the railroad continued on its westward trek, Prosperity lost some of its importance and much of its population. It was gradually beginning to recover though, and its hearty citizens hung on, waiting for the eventual bounty the railroad was sure to bring.

Two young men, passing through the town, stopped in front of the Red Bull Saloon. Swinging down from their horses, they patted their dusters down.

"Whoo-ee, Darrel, you're raising a cloud there like a summer dust storm," one of them said.

"Yeah, well, that gets rid of the dust from my coat, but there's only one way to get it out of my throat. And that's a cool, wet beer."

"You got that right," the first one said, laughing.

The two young men went into the saloon, then stepped up to the bar. The saloon was relatively quiet, with only four men at one table and a fifth standing down at the far end of the bar. The four at the table were playing cards; the one at the end of the bar was nursing a drink. The man nursing the drink was bald. He had a round, cannonball-shaped head and a prominent brow ridge, but no eyebrows. The head seemed to sit directly on his shoulders without benefit of a neck.

As the boys stepped up to the bar, the man with the cannonball head looked at them with an unblinking stare.

"What'll it be, gents?" the bartender asked.

One of the two boys stared back at the bald man.

"Billy?" Darrel said. "The bartender asked what'll we have."

"Oh," Billy said. "Uh, two beers."

"Two beers it is," the bartender replied. He turned to draw the beers.

"And I'll have the same," Darrel added.

The bartender laughed. "You boys sound like you've got a thirst."

"Yes, sir, we have," Billy said. "We have ridden hard for about six days now. Come up from Texas."

"Have you now?" the bartender replied. "That's a long ride. What brings you to Prosperity?"

"We're looking for a spread called Cross Pass," Darrel said. "We came here to meet with a gentleman by the name of Ian MacTavish. Do you know him?"

"What are you meeting with MacTavish about?" Cannonball asked.

"Excuse me, sir. Are you Mr. MacTavish?" Darrel asked.

"No."

"Then, no disrespect, mister, but I reckon what we're meeting with MacTavish about is between MacTavish and us."

The bartender put the beers in front of the two boys and they each picked up one.

"Did you say you came up from Texas?" Cannonball asked.

"Yes, sir, the great state of Texas," Darrel said. "Here's to Texas," he added, holding out his beer.

"I'd just as soon drink piss as drink a toast to Texas," Cannonball said.

Using the back of his hand, Billy wiped beer foam from his mouth. It was obvious that Cannonball had irritated him, and for the briefest of moments, that irritation reflected on his face. But he put it aside, then forced a smile.

"Hell, mister, if you don't like Texas, then all that means is that you just haven't seen the right part of it," Billy said. "Texas is so big, you have to find something about it you like."

"No, I don't," Cannonball said. "I don't like Texas and I don't like anyone who is from Texas."

Darrel had less patience than Billy. "You got something

stuck in your craw, mister?" he asked, bristling now at the man's comment. He turned away from the bar to face the man at the other end.

"Easy, Darrel," Billy said, reaching out for his partner. "I'm sure he doesn't mean anything personal by that remark. If he doesn't like Texas, he doesn't have to live there."

Darrel glared at Cannonball, but the expression on the man's face never changed.

"I just don't like being insulted by some roundheaded son of a bitch who doesn't know what he's talking about," Darrel said.

"We promised Colonel Galen we wouldn't get in no trouble, remember?" Billy said. "We're just up here to make a deal with Mr. MacTavish. That's all."

"*Colonel* Galen?" Cannonball asked. He laughed a short, mirthless laugh. "Would he be one of those Confederate colonels? As I recall, they gave that rank to just about everyone in the Confederate army, didn't they?"

"For your information, Colonel Galen holds his commission by authority of Victoria, Queen of England," Billy said.

"Victoria, Queen of England. You mean whore of England, don't you?"

"That's it, mister! I'm going to mop the floor with your sorry hide!" Darrel said. He put up his fists.

Cannonball smiled, a smile without mirth. "If we're going to fight, why don't we make it permanent?" he asked. He stepped away from the bar and flipped his jacket back, exposing a pistol that he wore low and kicked out, in the way of a gunfighter.

"Mr. Caulder, I'm sure these boys would apologize to you if you asked them for it," the bartender said. "There's no need to carry this any further."

"Caulder? James Caulder!" Billy suddenly exclaimed. "My God, Darrel, back off. Don't you know who this is?

This is the man they call the Widow Maker!"

Darrel realized now that he had been suckered into this, and he stopped, then opened his fists and held his hands, palm out, in front of him.

"Now, wait a minute!" he said. "Hold on! There's no need to carry things this far. This isn't worth either one of us dying over."

"Oh, it won't be *either* of us, sonny. It'll just be you," Cannonball said. "Both of you," he added, looking at Billy. "You came here together, you are going to die together."

"Neither my cousin nor I have any intention of drawing on you," Billy said. "If you shoot us, you are going to have to shoot us in cold blood, in front of these witnesses."

"What witnesses?" Caulder asked, looking toward the table where the card players had interrupted their game to watch the unfolding drama. "I don't see any witnesses."

Taking their cue, all four men got up from the table, two of them standing so quickly that their chairs fell over. The chairs struck the floor with two pops, as loud as gunshots, and both Billy and Darrel jumped. The four card players hurried out the front door, followed by the bartender. Billy's knees grew so weak that he could barely stand, and he felt nauseated.

"Please, Mr. Caulder, we don't want any trouble," Billy said. "Why don't you just let us apologize and we'll go on our way?"

Caulder shook his head. "You boys brought me to this ball, now you're goin' to have to dance with me," Caulder said. "Pull your guns."

"The sheriff," Darrel said. "How are you going to explain this to the sheriff?"

Smiling, Caulder turned the lapel of his jacket over. There, pinned to the back side of the lapel, was a sheriff's badge.

"I won't have any trouble at all," he said, his evil smile growing broader.

Billy and Darrel looked at each other, then, with an imperceptible signal, they started their draw. Though the two young men were able to defend themselves in most bar fights, they were badly overmatched in this fight. They made ragged, desperate grabs for their pistols.

So bad were they that Caulder had the luxury of waiting for just a moment to see which of the two offered him the most competition. Deciding it was Darrel, Caulder pulled his pistol and shot Darrel first. Billy, shocked at seeing his cousin killed right before his eyes, released his pistol and let it fall back into his holster. He was still looking at Darrel when Caulder's second shot, so close to the first one that some who were outside thought they heard only one report, hit Billy in the neck. He fell on top of Darrel.

Caulder walked through the cloud of gun smoke and quickly looked through the clothes of the two men he killed. In Billy's pocket he found an envelope from Colonel Galen addressed to Ian MacTavish. He took the envelope and put it in his own pocket, then walked back down to the end of the bar. He was calmly sipping his whiskey by the time a few of the citizens of the town got up the nerve to look inside.

Slocum waited for the train for three hours. When first he saw it, it was approaching at about twenty miles per hour, a respectable enough speed, though the vastness of the desert made it appear as if the train were going much slower. Against the great panorama of the desert the train seemed puny, and even the smoke that poured from its stack made but a tiny scar against the orange vault of sunset sky.

He could hear the train quite easily, the sound of its puffing engine carrying to him across the wide, flat ground the way sound travels across water. He stepped up onto the track and began waving. When he heard the steam valve close and the train begin braking, he knew that the engineer had spotted him and was going to stop. As the engine approached, it gave some perspective as to how large the desert really was, for the train that had appeared so tiny before was now a behemoth, blocking out the sky. It ground to a reluctant halt, its stack puffing black smoke, and its driver wheels wreathed in tendrils of white steam that purpled as they drifted away in the fading light.

The engineer's face appeared in the window and Slocum felt a prickly sensation as he realized that someone was holding a gun on him. He couldn't see it, but he knew that whoever it was—probably the fireman—had to be hiding in the tender.

"What do you want, mister? Why'd you stop us?" the engineer asked.

Slocum took his hat off and brushed his hair out of his eyes. The hair was lank, and grained like oak, worn trail-weary long, just over his ears. With it repositioned, he put his hat, sweat-stained and well-worn, back on his head.

"I had to put my horse down," Slocum explained. "I need a ride."

The engineer studied him for a moment as if trying to ascertain whether or not Slocum represented any danger to him or to his passengers. Finally he decided it would be safe to pick up this stranger.

"All right," the engineer said. "A dollar will get you to Prosperity. We'll be there in about two more hours. Take the second car. The first car is a private car, belonging to Cross Pass."

"Thanks," Slocum said. He picked up the saddle and started toward the rear of the train. "Oh, and you can tell your fireman it's all right to come out now."

"What the hell? How did you know I was in here?" the fireman's muffled voice called.

Slocum knew because his very life often depended upon his ability to understand such things.

The private car was the first car behind the tender. It was a beautifully varnished car, bearing a brass plaque with the words Cross Pass Station. As he walked by the car he saw the curtains part, and a woman's face appeared in one of the windows. It was the face of a middle-aged woman, with gray-streaked hair and the clear skin of someone much younger. She had penetrating blue eyes, and she appraised Slocum in frank curiosity, refusing to look away when Slocum looked back at her.

When Slocum reached the first car just behind the private car, he threw his saddle up onto the deck of the vestibule then climbed up and stepped inside. There were a couple of dozen passengers in the car—men, women, and children—and they all looked up in curiosity at the man who had caused the train to stop in the middle of the desert. Slocum touched the brim of his hat, then walked to the last seat on the right and settled into it. He pulled his legs up so that his knees were resting on the seatback in front of him, reached up and casually tipped his hat forward, then folded his arms across his chest. Within moments, he was sound asleep.

Juanita Arino was returning to Prosperity after a visit with her sister. She was sitting across the aisle from the seat the stranger took when he boarded the train. She thought it very curious that he would get on the train in the middle of the desert, and she wished she had the courage to ask him about it. But she would never disturb him; he was too fearsome-looking for that.

She watched him in the fading light as he drifted off to sleep. He was fearsome, yes, but she found herself strangely attracted to that fearsomeness, and she wondered what it would be like to be with him.

Scolding herself for such a thought, she leaned back in her seat and looked through the window, listening to the rhythmic clack of the wheels over rail joints.

She wasn't sure when it started, she knew only that an unknown man's hands were touching her breasts and rubbing her nipples until, like tiny, budding blooms, they rose in response. Then those same hands explored her smooth skin to the dimple of her navel before moving farther down, across the curve of her thighs, and on to her most private part. He followed his hands with his mouth, caressing and kissing the inside of her thighs, then his tongue stabbed into her, sending dizzying charges of pleasure through her entire body. Writhing in delight, she reached down to put her hands on the back of his head and spread her legs wide to pull him into her. It wasn't until then that he looked up and she saw that the man who was lifting her to such dizzying heights of ecstasy was the stranger who had just boarded the train.

"Señor, what are you doing?" she gasped.

Suddenly Juanita was wide awake and she sat bolt upright in her seat, breathing heavily, looking around the car, wondering if she had spoken out loud. Evidently she had not, for no one seemed to be paying any attention to her. She looked over at the man who had recently boarded and saw that he was still sleeping.

Juanita's skin was flushed, she was sweating, and her heart was racing. Even more disturbing was the moist, tingling sensation she was feeling between her legs. She squeezed her fists so tightly that her fingernails bit into the palms of her hands. Only then could she make the disturbing images of her dream go away.

"Who do you think it is, Aunt Emma?" Julie MacTavish asked. Julie was tall and slender with copper hair and green eyes.

"Who is who, dear?" Emma answered, looking up from her reading.

"The man who got onto the train."

Emma chuckled. "Heavens, dear, have you been thinking about him all this time?"

"No. Well, not exactly. I'm just curious, that's all. Don't you think it is curious the way he boarded the train, right out here in the middle of nowhere?"

"I'm sure he is just someone who needed a ride. If you noticed, he was carrying a saddle. If I were going to guess, I would say his horse went lame."

"Yes, that's probably it. He was good-looking, don't you think? In a rugged sort of way, I mean?"

Emma MacTavish chuckled. "Now what makes you think, at my age, I would notice things like that?"

"Your age? Aunt Emma, you may be older, but you aren't dead. And you certainly noticed Uncle Ian."

"Yes, I did notice your uncle Ian," Emma agreed with a smile.

2

The train had been under way for about an hour and a half when it came to a sudden, shuddering, screeching, banging halt. It stopped so abruptly that some of the passengers were thrown from their seats, including a young boy who began crying.

Slocum woke with a start and looked through the window. Coal-oil lanterns mounted on gimbals lit the inside of the car, and their reflection on the windows made it even more difficult to see in the dark outside.

"What is it?" someone asked.

"Are we going to stop at every rock and cranny in this entire desert?" another wanted to know.

"I nearly broke my neck! The railroad is certainly going to hear from me!" a man complained.

Though he couldn't see anything, Slocum heard loud, guttural voices outside and surmised at once what was gong on. He pulled his pistol from his holster, let it rest on his knee, then covered it with his hat.

"Everyone stay in their seats!" a man shouted, bursting into the car from the front. He wore a bandanna tied across the bottom half of his face and he held a pistol that

11

he pointed toward the passengers in the car.

"Señor Cole!" Juanita said quietly.

Slocum heard the pretty Mexican girl's exclamation and he looked over at her curiously. He saw her slink down in her seat, then pull her shawl up around her head, obviously trying not to be seen by the gunman.

"See here! What is this?" a man shouted indignantly. He started to get up, but the gunman moved quickly toward him and brought his pistol down sharply over the man's head. The passenger groaned and fell back. A woman who had been sitting with him cried out in alarm.

"Anybody else?" the gunman challenged. "Maybe you folks didn't hear me when I said everyone stay in their seats."

Another gunman came in to join the first. "What happened?" he asked.

"Nothing I can't handle. Is everything under control out there?"

"Yeah," the second gunman answered. "Ever'one is doin' just what you told 'em. Lou is coverin' the engineer, Sam is unhookin' the train."

"Why don't we just wear signs hangin' around our necks, tellin' folks who we are?" the first gunman asked, angrily.

"I'm sorry, Pete! I guess I just wasn't thinkin'!"

"You dumb bastard, you did it again!"

"Sorry."

"Never mind, just keep everyone in here covered. I'm going outside to make certain everything is going like it should."

"How will I know when you're pullin' the private car away? I mean, what if you fellas leave and I don't know you're gone? I'll be stuck back here."

"We'll blow the whistle before we go," Pete said as he left.

Once Pete left, the new gunman, as if suddenly hitting

upon the idea, took his hat off and began passing down the aisle. "Folks," he said. "What I want you to do is put all your money and valuables in this hat. If you try and hold out on me, I'll shoot you."

He started down the aisle making his collection and though a few people grumbled, no one held back until he reached the row where Slocum and the pretty Mexican girl were sitting across the aisle from each other. Slocum noticed that she had pulled the shawl completely up over her head now, and was looking toward the window.

"Lookin' away from me ain't goin' to do you no good," the gunman said gruffly to Juanita. "Look around here."

She didn't move.

The gunman started to reach for her. "I said, look around at me!" he demanded in a louder voice.

"Leave the girl alone," Slocum said.

The gunman looked over at Slocum. "What did you say?"

"I said leave the girl alone."

"What the hell, mister? You think you're giving orders here?" the train robber asked. "I'm the one giving the orders here. And while we're at it, just put all your money in this hat."

"I've got a better idea," Slocum said. "You put the hat down and leave the car. If you do that, I'll let you live."

"You'll what?" The gunman's laugh was a high-pitched cackle. "You'll let *me* live? Are you crazy?"

"Do what I said, or die," Slocum said, calmly.

Suddenly the train robber perceived that Slocum meant business, and he pulled the hammer back on his pistol. That was as far as he got before Slocum pulled the trigger on his own gun, which he was holding under his hat. He blew a hole in his hat, but more importantly, opened up a hole in the robber's chest. Dropping his gun, the robber clutched his chest, and staggered back a few steps.

The gunshot caused everyone in the car to scream, and

the girl across the aisle from Slocum looked around at the robber. Slocum saw a look of horror on the girl's face, coupled with a look of recognition on the face of the gunman.

The gunman pointed to the girl. "You! What are you . . ." That was as far as he got before he fell.

"Barry! What is it?" Pete asked, jumping back onto the train. Seeing Barry down and Slocum standing, Pete realized quickly what was going on, more quickly, even, than Slocum would have thought. Pete fired at Slocum but his shot went wide and the bullet smashed through the window beside John's seat, sending out a stinging spray of glass but doing no other damage. Slocum brought his own pistol up and squeezed off a second shot. Pete staggered back, his hands to his throat. Blood spilled through his fingers as he hit the front wall of the car, then slid down to the floor in a seated position. His arms fell to either side as he died.

During the gunfire women screamed and men shouted. As the car filled with the gun smoke of three discharges, Slocum scooted out through the back door of the car, jumped from the steps down to the ground, then fell and rolled out into the darkness.

"Pete! Barry! What's going on in there?" someone called. "What's going on?"

In the dim light that spilled through the car windows, Slocum saw the gunman who was yelling at the others. This was the one who had been covering the engineer, so he knew it must be Lou. The robber was moving quickly toward the back of the train. As Lou ran through the little golden patches of light it had the effect of a lantern blinking on and off so that first he was in shadow, then brightly illuminated, then in shadow, then illuminated again. Slocum aimed at him.

"Hold it right there, Lou!" Slocum called out to him.

"I've got you covered. Put down your gun and throw up your hands."

"What the hell?" Lou responded. He suddenly realized he was in a patch of light and moved quickly into the shadow to fire at John. Lou may have thought he had found safety in the darkness, but the two-foot-wide muzzle flash of his pistol gave Slocum an ideal target and Slocum returned fire. Lou's bullet whistled by harmlessly, but Slocum's bullet found its mark and Lou let out a little yell, grabbed his chest, then collapsed.

Slocum stood up then, and moved toward the side of the train to try to get a bead on the one who had been disconnecting the rest of the train from the private car. Slocum saw him then, just as he was stepping through the door and into the private car. Slocum snapped off a shot but missed. He saw his bullet send up sparks as it struck part of the metal in the door frame. He didn't get a second shot because the outlaw made it inside.

"Get out of my car!" Emma MacTavish said when the outlaw stepped inside.

"Shut up, you old crone!" Sam said, pointing his pistol at her. Looking around the dimly lit car, he saw Julie sitting in an overstuffed chair near one window. He whistled. "You rich people really know how to travel, don't you?"

"What are you going to do?" Julie asked in a frightened tone of voice.

"I'm going to shoot the both of you, if you don't do exactly what I say," Sam answered. He walked over to the window and, pulling the curtain to one side, looked out.

Slocum had hurried to the front of the passenger car, then backed up against the side of it so the robber, who was now safely inside the private car, wouldn't have a clear shot at him. One of the passengers poked his head out to see what was going on.

"Get back inside!" Slocum shouted gruffly. "You want your fool head shot off?"

The passenger jerked his head back in quickly.

Slocum peered cautiously around the corner, trying to see his adversary.

"Sam!" he called, remembering the name. "Sam, you may as well come on out of there. There's nowhere for you to go. Pete, Barry, and Lou are dead. I killed them. You're the only one left."

"How . . . how the hell do you know our names?" Sam called back. "Who the hell are you?"

"I'm the man who is going to kill you, if you don't come out," Slocum said. "You better listen to me. I promise you, you aren't going to get away."

"A name," Sam called back. "Give me your name."

"The name's Slocum. John Slocum."

"Yeah? Well, I never heard of you, John Slocum."

Inside the car, Sam looked back at Emma MacTavish. "Who is this fella, Slocum? Is he a hired gun you and your husband brought in here?"

"He could be," Emma said easily.

"Son of a bitch!" Sam said. "Draper said this was going to be easy!"

"How long have you worked for Draper, that you haven't learned he is a lying bastard?" Emma asked.

Sam looked through the window again.

"Slocum? Slocum, you still out there?"

"I'm still here."

"I'm comin' out," Sam said. "Don't shoot, I'm comin' out."

"That's more like it," Slocum replied.

Sam looked around the car, his eyes, like the eyes of a trapped rat, beady and frightened-looking. He reached over and grabbed Emma and jerked her to him.

"What are you doing?" Emma shouted in surprise and fear.

"I'm buyin' myself a little insurance," Sam said. He wrapped his arm around her neck.

Slocum watched the back door of the private car. A second later it opened, and true to his promise, Sam came out. But he didn't come out alone. He had his arm around Emma MacTavish's neck, and he was holding the barrel of his pistol against her temple.

"You still out there, Slocum?" Sam called, searching the darkness. "You still here?"

"I'm here," Slocum answered quietly, so close to Sam that it startled him. "Let her go, Sam."

Sam gasped at the closeness. "Like hell I'll let her go," he replied. "Mrs. MacTavish is my ticket out of here. I'll let her go when I know I'm somewhere safe."

"You aren't going anywhere."

"The hell I'm not. Don't you understand? If you don't back off, I'm going to blow her brains out."

"No, you don't understand," Slocum said. "I don't care whether you blow her brains out or not. In the meantime, you've made a bad mistake. Your gun is pointed at that woman, my gun is pointed at you."

"Damn right it's pointed at this woman!" Sam said, desperately trying to explain the situation. "What's the matter with you? Are you stupid or something? I'm going to shoot her if you don't back off."

"Shoot her," Slocum said laconically.

"What are you talking about? This is Emma Mac-Tavish. Do you understand what I'm saying to you? This is Emma MacTavish of Cross Pass Station."

"Never heard of her, never heard of Cross Pass Station," Slocum said, easily. "Put your gun down, Sam. It's the only way you are going to get out of here alive."

"No, it ain't the only way," Sam said, trying again. "Like I told you, I got me this here ace up my sleeve."

"You've got nothing."

"Goddamnit, listen to what I'm telling you, you dumb son of a bitch! I am going to shoot this woman!" Sam yelled, as if yelling it would make Slocum understand.

"All right, go ahead, just quit talking about it. Shoot her and get it over with so you and I can get down to business."

"What?" Sam asked, shocked by the answer he hadn't expected to hear.

"I said go ahead. Do it. Shoot her," Slocum said. "If she's lived a pretty good life, she'll probably go to heaven. I'll be sending you directly to hell."

"You're bluffing."

"Why would I be bluffing?" Slocum asked. "I told you, I don't know the woman. All I want is for her to be out of the way so you and I can get down to business. In fact, if you don't shoot her by the time I count to five, I'll shoot her myself. Then I'll shoot you." Slocum moved the barrel of his gun slightly so that he was now aiming at the woman. Slowly and deliberately, he cocked his pistol. "One," he said.

"You son of a bitch!" Sam yelled.

"Two." John's voice was slow, quiet, and deliberate.

"My God! You're crazy! You are really crazy!"

"Three."

Sam pulled his gun away from the woman's head so he could aim at Slocum. Quickly and smoothly, Slocum moved his sight to a new target and squeezed the trigger. The gun boomed and bucked in his hand, and his bullet whizzed by within an inch of Emma MacTavish's head, hitting Sam right between the eyes. The impact of the heavy bullet threw Sam back against the door of the car, then he collapsed in a heap onto the vestibule floor. Emma MacTavish never said a word, though she did jump involuntarily as Sam fell behind her.

"You all right, ma'am?"

"Yes, young man, I'm fine," Emma said.

"No thanks to you!" Julie said angrily, stepping into the door.

"What happened?" someone yelled.

"Is it all over?" another asked.

There were sounds of footfalls as several people ran up to the car.

"Drop that gun, mister," the conductor said, pointing a rifle at Slocum.

"Better do what he says," a passenger from one of the other cars ordered. The passenger was also armed, and, like the conductor, was pointing his gun at Slocum. "We've both got you covered."

"So have I," a third said.

"Nonsense, what are you men doing?" Emma asked. "Didn't you see what happened here? Don't you people realize that Mr. Slocum just saved my life? He probably saved a great many lives tonight. Put your guns down, all of you."

"You're sure you're all right, Mrs. MacTavish?" the conductor asked.

"Yes, I'm positive. Now, please, get someone up here to get this terrible man's wretched body off my car."

"Yes, ma'am," the conductor replied. "You fellas, climb up there and get him."

"There are two more in here," one of the passengers said. "This fella killed both of them."

"I nearly stumbled over one lying out here in the dark," one of the armed passengers said.

"Good Lord, how many did you kill?" the conductor asked.

"Four," Slocum answered without elaboration.

"How many were there?"

"There were four," the engineer said, coming up then. "I seen 'em when I stopped the train."

"Why in heaven's name did you stop?" the conductor asked the engineer.

"There's a barricade on the track ahead. If I hadn't stopped, we would've run off the track," the engineer explained.

"All right, those of you who aren't collecting bodies, help clear the track," the conductor ordered.

"Where do we put the bodies?"

"Throw them on the rear vestibule of the last car," the conductor said. "You," he said to Slocum. He sighed. "I'm sorry I accused you. I reckon we owe you a debt of gratitude. Climb on back into your car, I'll see to it that the railroad refunds the cost of your ticket."

Slocum laughed.

"What is it?"

"I only paid a dollar for passage to Prosperity. That means the railroad has just agreed to pay a bounty of twenty-five cents a head for the men I killed."

"I can do a little better than that," Emma said.

Slocum held up his hand. "No, ma'am, I'm not after any bounty money from you."

"I'm not talking about bounty money," Emma said. "I'm talking about spending the rest of the trip in my private car, with my niece and me."

"Well, I . . ."

"And a drink?"

Slocum hesitated.

"I'm not talking about elderberry wine, young man. I'm talking about sipping whiskey. Good sipping whiskey," she added with a twinkle in her eye.

"Uh, Mrs. MacTavish," the conductor said. "You sure you want to do that? We don't know anything about this man."

"I agree with the conductor, Aunt Emma," Julie said. "After all, he told that man to shoot you. He even said that he would shoot you if that man didn't."

"Yes, and a brilliant move it was, too," Emma said. "Come in please, Mr. Slocum."

"Thank you," Slocum said. "Maybe I will take you up on it."

"What won you over? The sipping whiskey, or the opportunity to spend some time with my niece?"

Slocum looked at the conductor. "I think the fact that you still invited me, even after he advised you against it."

Emma laughed, then she looked over at the conductor. "Carl, how much longer until we reach Prosperity?"

"About an hour, I guess."

"Tell Hank I'll give him a dollar a minute for every minute under an hour it takes to get us there. In fact, I'll give a dollar a minute to the entire train crew."

The conductor smiled broadly. "Yes, ma'am," he said. "Uh, I'd better go up ahead and help clear the track."

3

"Have a seat, sir," Emma said, once Slocum was in the car.

Slocum took the seat he was offered, an overstuffed chair that would have made a handsome addition to any drawing room in any house in the country.

"Mr. Slocum, is it?" Julie asked.

"Yes, ma'am."

"I have to tell you that I don't share my aunt Emma's enthusiastic support of you. I believe you really would have shot her."

"Yes."

"Yes? Yes, what?"

"I intended you to believe I would have shot her."

"Would you have?"

"I didn't."

"That's not the question," Julie said in exasperation. "The question I asked you is, would you have shot her?"

"Did it rain yesterday?" Slocum asked.

"What?" Julie replied, shocked by the unexpected question.

"Did it rain yesterday?" Slocum asked again.

"What does that have to do with anything?"

"That's my point."

Julie let out a long, frustrated "Oooooh," but Emma enjoyed a hearty laugh.

"Julie, give it up, darling," she said.

The engineer blew his whistle, then the train started forward with a few jerks.

"Oh, good, we are under way," Emma said.

"He still hasn't answered my question," Julie said.

"Darling, a man as cool and collected as Mr. Slocum is isn't going to give away any of his secrets. The point is, he made the outlaw believe he was going to shoot me, and, under the circumstances, that was absolutely necessary. I am also happy to report that he did not shoot me, and that is what is important. Now, quit being disagreeable, and help me entertain our guest." Emma poured whiskey from a sculptured glass decanter into a crystal glass, then handed it to Julie. "Take this glass to him."

"Yes, ma'am," Julie said contritely, receiving the glass from her aunt Emma. She took it over to John.

"Thank you," Slocum said, taking the glass.

As the train wheels clacked rhythmically beneath him, Slocum noticed that Mrs. MacTavish's private car rocked much more gently than the rough riding car he had been on. And this at the noticeably increased speed.

Slocum sipped the whiskey. Over the course of his life, Slocum had drunk just about every type of alcohol available in every flyblown hellhole from the Mexican border to the Dakota Badlands. He had drunk beer that was so green he could still taste the yeast, and whiskey that was aged with rusty nails and flavored with tobacco juice. Once he had even drunk champagne, but he had never tasted anything like the "sipping whiskey" he was drinking now.

"Do you like it?" Emma asked.

"Yes, ma'am," Slocum said. His answer wasn't adequate to express how much he really did like it, but he never was a man for words.

"It comes directly from Scotland," Emma said. "My husband says it is the morning mist, bottled right from the Scottish moors. Do you agree?"

Slocum shrugged and Emma laughed.

"I'm teasing," she said. "I don't know what the hell he means by that either. But he is a very poetic man, my husband, and he came to America from a fine, old, Scottish family, back before the war. He built Cross Pass Station. I heard you tell the gunman that you had no idea what Cross Pass Station was. Is that true? You've never heard of it?"

"No, ma'am, I haven't."

"Well, for your enlightenment, young man, Cross Pass Station is a cattle ranch. And not just any cattle ranch, mind you. It is a huge ranch with thousands of acres of grassland and water, and thousands of fat cows. Then, after my husband built Cross Pass Station, he was like Adam in the Garden of Eden. And, like Adam, decided that he needed to take unto himself a wife. That's where I came in. He went to San Francisco to see the sights and he saw me. Your glass is empty. Pour him another, Julie."

"Yes, ma'am," Julie replied. She brought the decanter of whiskey over and refilled John's glass. This time she actually smiled at him. Evidently her aunt Emma's acceptance of Slocum had softened Julie's attitude as well.

"My husband is a lord, actually. If we were in Scotland, I would be a lady." She laughed out loud. "But of course, we aren't in Scotland so I have no illusions as to what I am."

"You don't have to be in Scotland to be a lady, Mrs. MacTavish," Slocum said. "It's clear to anyone that you are a fine lady."

"Well, aren't you the gentlemen though?" Emma said, laughing. "The truth is, I could have been a fine lady. I started out that way. I was born in Georgia to a fine, old family, but I came west with my first husband. He had fine plans, he did. But, he caught a fever and died and I was stranded. At the time there was only one way a woman could make a living and I think you are smart enough to figure out what that was."

"Aunt Emma!" Julie said in a shocked voice.

"Darlin'," Emma said. "I expect Mr. Slocum has known more than a few women who have hiked their skirts for pay. And if he has, he knows to judge them by who they are, and not what they are. Am I right, Mr. Slocum?"

"You are right, Mrs. MacTavish. But please call me John."

"Tell me, John, what brings you to Prosperity?" Emma asked.

"A dead horse."

"What an odd answer," Julie said.

"Odd, perhaps, but true," Slocum said. He explained how he was forced to shoot his horse, then walk several miles to connect with the railroad in order to avoid being stranded in the desert.

"What are you going to do in Prosperity?"

"Buy a horse, for one thing. Maybe look around for a card game or two. And I'm going to check on those four train robbers. I'm not a bounty hunter, but if there is any paper on them, I intend to collect the reward."

"You won't find any paper on them," Emma said.

"There must be. People who rob trains have an outlaw background that catches up with them."

"There are two things wrong with that observation," Emma said. "For one thing they weren't trying to rob the train, they were trying to capture me. And for another, even if they do have an outlaw background, which I'm sure they do, you won't find any paper on them because the sheriff in Prosperity has taken care of it."

"The sheriff?"

"A despicable man," Julie said. "One only has to be around him to smell a hint of sulfur. And he is so ugly, with that round, bald head, no hair anywhere, not even eyebrows or eyelashes.

"He can't help how he looks, dear. Only how he acts."

"This man you are describing. Would his name be Caulder? James Caulder?"

"Yes. You know him?"

"I know him," Slocum said.

"I hope we haven't offended you by what we have said about him. I mean if he is a friend of yours . . ."

"The Widow Maker is no friend of mine," Slocum said quickly.

"The Widow Maker, yes, that is what they call him. He is our sheriff now, replacing a good and decent man who was fired by the mayor. The mayor and some of the city council are in Draper's pocket."

"Some of?"

"Yes, just some. Prosperity is a good town, Mr. Slocum. Or at least, it was, before Draper arrived and began turning things sour."

"I take it you don't like Draper."

"No, sir, I do not. Right now, Draper and my husband are in a dispute."

"What is the dispute over?"

"What else would it be out here? It's over land. You see, Draper has bought up most of the smaller ranches and added their acreage to his own so that, in terms of acres, Crown Ranch is now the biggest ranch in the territory."

"I thought Cross Pass was."

"Cross Pass is more productive than Crown Ranch, and Draper wants it. That's why he sent those men to get me."

"You think he sent those men?"

"Of course he sent them. I knew those men, every one of them," Emma said. "They worked for Seth Draper."

"They were pretty well-known, were they?" Slocum asked. "By that, I mean most of the people of town would recognize them if they saw them?"

"Yes."

"That explains it, then."

"Explains what?"

"There was a girl back in the car I was riding in, a pretty Mexican señorita. She seemed to know them. And, just before one of them died, I got the impression he knew her."

"A Mexican girl?" Emma asked.

"That would be Juanita, Aunt Emma. I saw her just before we boarded the train back in Risco."

"Oh, yes, her sister lives in Risco."

"Who is Juanita?" Slocum asked.

"Juanita Arino," Emma said. "She works for Draper."

"She's his maid, but she is as decent a young woman as you'll ever hope to meet," Julie added quickly. "She has nothing to do with any of his evil shenanigans."

At that moment the train began slowing, and Julie looked through the window curtain. "We're coming into Prosperity," she said.

Emma took a watch from her reticule and examined it. "Oh, we made very good time. It looks as if I'm going to have to pay the bonus I promised."

"Is this the end of the line for you?" Slocum asked.

"It is, as far as Western Pacific Railroad is concerned. But we have a private spur line that runs from town out to Cross Pass. However, there won't be a switch engine available to take us out there until tomorrow afternoon, so yes, we will be getting off here tonight."

Slocum stood up. "I'll be getting off here as well. I'd like to thank you for the whiskey and for letting me ride in your car."

"You are very welcome," Emma said. "By the way, do you have any idea where you will be staying tonight?"

"No, I've never been in this town."

"We keep several rooms at the New Congress Hotel. We will stay there tonight, before going out to the ranch tomorrow. You are very welcome to use one of our rooms."

"Well, I appreciate the offer, but . . ."

"There is no obligation, John, I assure you. The New Congress also happens to be the best hotel in town and, since you are going to have to stay somewhere, you may as well stay in the best. Especially since it is free."

Slocum smiled. "All right," he said. "Thanks. Maybe, after I've taken care of a little business, I'll take you up on that."

"See the desk clerk when you come in. He'll have a key waiting for you."

"Ma'am," Slocum said touching his hat. Then, to Julie. "Miss MacTavish. I'll be seeing you." He stepped out of the train and down onto the wooden platform of the Prosperity depot.

Behind Slocum, the train, temporarily at rest from its long run, wasn't quiet. Because the engineer kept the steam up, the valve continued to open and close in great, heaving sighs. Overheated wheel bearings and gearboxes popped and snapped as tortured metal cooled. On the platform all around him, there was a discordant chorus of squeals, laughter, shouts, and animated conversation as people were getting on and off the train.

When Slocum looked toward the rear of the train, he saw that the four bodies were being taken down from the last car and laid out side by side at the far end of the platform. Already the curious were beginning to gather around the bodies, and by the time Slocum got his saddle and made arrangements to leave it in the baggage room of the depot, there were more than two dozen people.

"Did you see the bodies they took off the train?" the

baggage clerk asked as he got out a yellow tag to tie to Slocum's saddle.

"Yeah," Slocum answered. "I saw them."

"There's going to be hell to pay over this," the clerk said. "Yes, sir, hell to pay. Those men worked for Mr. Draper."

"Tell me about Draper." Slocum had heard a little about Draper from Emma MacTavish, but of course that was only one side. As much as possible, he liked to know both sides of a dispute, or at least one side and a neutral side.

"He's the biggest landowner in the territory. Crown Ranch is even bigger than Cross Pass. I reckon you've heard of Cross Pass, haven't you?"

"Yes, I have."

"Of course there was a time when Mr. MacTavish owned the biggest spread. Fact is, he owned just about all the land around here then. He's Scottish, you know."

"So I've heard. Was Cross Pass bigger than Crown Ranch?"

The clerk chuckled. "Hell, MacTavish owned Crown Ranch, too. Only it wasn't Crown Ranch then. It was all just a part of his spread. Folks say that in its heyday, Cross Pass was bigger'n most states and some countries."

"If MacTavish used to own it, how did Draper come by Crown Ranch?"

"Draper showed up in court one day with some old Spanish land grants that he claims to have bought from the Bustamante family. Everyone knows that all this land belonged to the Bustamantes at one time. But the Spanish pulled out of here nearly a hundred years ago. Seems like the only thing they were after was gold, and when they didn't find any of that, they weren't interested anymore."

"So the land was empty when MacTavish arrived?"

"Not just MacTavish. When people began coming here from back East, they were told that if they filed on the land, and made improvements, it would be theirs. But, somehow, Draper got the judge to honor those old Spanish grants so the court carved away several thousand acres from MacTavish and gave them to Draper. Didn't pay him nothin' for it, either. Then, after that, Draper started addin' land so that now Crown Ranch is bigger'n it ever was."

"Draper sounds like an ambitious man."

"He is that," the clerk said. "And he's a fella you don't want to cross."

"Where's the sheriff's office?"

"You got business with the sheriff?" the clerk asked, his curiosity plainly evident.

"Where is his office?" Slocum asked again, purposely avoiding the clerk's question.

"It's down the street," the clerk answered. "But if you're lookin' for Sheriff Caulder, you'll more'n likely find him down there with those four dead men."

"Thanks," Slocum said.

"I must say, this has been quite a day," the clerk said. "First, the two men Sheriff Caulder killed, then these four men. Yes, sir, it's been quite a day for Prosperity."

"Caulder killed two men today?"

"Yes, we had quite a shoot-out down at the saloon this afternoon. A couple of Texas cowboys made the mistake of trying to outdraw Sheriff Caulder, and they died for their trouble. I hope neither of them was married. Sheriff Caulder isn't called the Widow Maker for nothing, you know."

4

Leaving the clerk's office, Slocum walked down to the
far end of the depot platform where the bodies had been
laid out as if on display. Each one had his arms folded
across his chest. Three of them had their eyes open. The
only exception was Sam, whose eyelid muscles had been
destroyed by the bullet that hit him right between the eyes.
Among a dozen or more who were standing there looking
down at the bodies, Slocum saw the albino.

"There he is, Sheriff," someone said. "That's the fella
that done it. He took all four of 'em on. It was quite a
thing to see."

Caulder stared at Slocum through narrowed, browless
eyes. It was obvious to Slocum that the sheriff was trying
to remember where they had met. It was a long time ago.
Caulder was a bounty hunter then, a regulator who would
rather bring in dead quarry than live prisoners. Two of
the men he brought in had been friends of Slocum's,
falsely accused. And, although the reward had been with-
drawn and they had been cleared, some old paper was still
out. Caulder was acting on that old paper when he hunted
them down and killed both of them. When he brought

31

them in for the reward, only to learn that there was no reward, Caulder's only reaction was frustration, not remorse. Only the fact that all the paper hadn't been pulled prevented him from being charged with murder.

Slocum had identified the bodies. Because there was nothing remarkable in Slocum's appearance, he didn't expect Caulder to remember him. But Slocum could never forget the bounty hunter who had killed his friends.

"Do I know you, mister?" Caulder asked.

"I doubt it."

Caulder stared at him a moment longer, as if trying to dredge up a memory from long past. When he couldn't, he returned to the job at hand.

"You killed these men?" Caulder asked.

"Yes."

"Why?"

"They were trying to kill me."

"I know these men, and that's hard for me to believe. I'll be honest with you, mister, if there was any way I could charge you with murder, I would. But I've got a whole train full of witnesses who swear you did kill them in self-defense. So there's nothing I can do about it."

"I'd like to check your dodgers," Slocum said.

"You a bounty hunter?"

"No. But if there was any reward for them, I aim to collect."

"You'll find nothing. If there was any paper out on them, I would have known about it, and I would've picked them up a long time ago."

"Maybe there's a reward out for them that you don't know about," Slocum suggested.

"I doubt it."

"Check."

Caulder sighed. "I guess I can send a telegram up to the capital tomorrow morning," he said. "If you want to stick around until then."

"I've got no place else to go. I'll drop by and see you in the morning."

"I'll be out of my office tomorrow. You can see Percy," Caulder said. "He's my deputy."

Slocum walked down the street from the depot toward the town. The Red Bull was the most substantial-looking saloon in a row of saloons. There was a drunk passed out on the steps in front of the place and Slocum had to step over him in order to go inside.

Because all the chimneys of all the lanterns were soot-covered, what light there was was dingy and filtered through drifting smoke. The place smelled of whiskey, stale beer, and sour tobacco. There was a long bar on the left, with dirty towels hanging on hooks about every five feet along its front. A large mirror was behind the bar, but like everything else about the saloon, it was so dirty that Slocum could scarcely see any images in it, and what he could see was distorted by imperfections in the glass.

Over against the back wall, near the foot of the stairs, a cigar-scarred, beer-stained upright piano was being played by a bald-headed musician. The tune was *Buffalo Gals*, and one of the girls who was a buffalo gal stood alongside, swaying to the music. Slocum was once told that this song was now very popular back East, and was often sung by the most genteel ladies. The easterners had no idea that the term buffalo gal referred to doxies who, during the rapid expansion of the railroad, had to ply their trade on buffalo robes, thrown out on the ground. This was because there were few buildings and fewer beds.

Out on the floor of the saloon, nearly all the tables were filled. A half dozen or so buffalo gals were flitting about, pushing drinks and promising more than they really intended to deliver. A few card games were in progress, but most of the patrons were just drinking and talking. The subject of their conversation was the gunfight that had taken place in the saloon earlier in the day. Now, however, they had also heard of the gunfight that took place on the train, so there was speculation as to which of the two shooters was the best.

"In my mind there ain't no doubt," one of the men at one of the tables was saying. "That fella on the train took on four men. Four, mind you, and he killed all of them. You can't compare that with the Widow Maker just killin' two men."

"The hell you can't," another man contended. "That fella on the train done his killin' in the dark. Caulder done his killin' in broad daylight. He called two men out and stood up to them, face to face."

"They wasn't gunfighters, they was cowboys."

"They was Texans, wasn't they? Hell, ever'body in Texas fancies hisself bein' a gunfighter, don't they?"

"Fancyin' yourself being a gunfighter and actual being one is two different things."

"Still, standin' up to two of 'em, face to face."

"You know what I'd like to see," one of the conversationalists said. "What I'd like to see is Sheriff Caulder go up against that fella that took on them train robbers."

"Whoo-ee! Wouldn't that purely be somethin' to behold, though?"

The bartender was pouring the residue from abandoned whiskey glasses back into a bottle when Slocum stepped up to the bar. The bartender pulled a soggy cigar butt from one glass, laid the butt aside, then poured the whiskey back into the bottle. Slocum held up his finger.

"Yeah, can I help you?"

Slocum thought of ordering a whiskey, considered what he had just seen, and remembering the sipping whiskey he had on the train, didn't want to erase that memory just yet. "A beer," he said.

The bartender turned to the beer barrel, pulled the spigot handle, and filled a mug. He slid the mug across the bar to Slocum. "That'll be a nickel," he said.

"I'd like it in a clean glass."

"A clean glass? Kind of highfalutin, aren't you?"

"Jeb?" a nearby customer called.

Jeb held his hand out toward the customer, indicating he wasn't yet finished with his discussion.

"Everyone else uses the mug I give them. What makes you any different from them?"

"Jeb?" the customer said again with a little more urgency.

Jeb picked up the mug. "Now, if you want it, give me your nickel. Otherwise, this goes back in the barrel."

"Jeb!" the customer yelled this time.

"What the hell do you want, Smitty? Can't you see I'm busy here?"

"Come here," Smitty said.

Still holding the beer, Jeb walked down the bar to the insistent customer. The customer whispered something in Jeb's ear, and Jeb blanched visibly. Quickly, he poured the beer he was holding into a slop bucket, then got another mug and showed it to Slocum.

"What about this mug? Is it clean enough?" he asked solicitously.

"That'll do," Slocum said.

"You should'a said somethin'," the bartender said as, with a shaking hand, he held a new mug under the beer spigot. "You should'a tol' me you was the one who killed them fellas on the train."

All conversation halted as the entire saloon looked at the man who had been one of the subjects of their discussion. Slocum looked over the room coldly and without comment. Then he slapped his nickel on the bar and reached for his beer.

"No, sir, your money is no good in here," Jeb said. "The beer is on the house for savin' the train like you done."

"Thanks," Slocum said picking up the nickel and pocketing it. He drank the beer in about three long drinks, then set the empty mug on the bar. "Can a fella get anything to eat in here?"

"Bacon, beans, and fried taters," Jeb said.

"Leave off the beans. Biscuits?"

"Best you ever ate," Jeb said. "My wife bakes 'em."

"Sounds good. With another beer."

Supper was pretty good, though Slocum was certain that his hunger was the predominant spice. After supper, Slocum left the saloon.

"Yes, sir," he heard someone say as he stepped through the bat-wing doors. "That fella there and the Widow Maker goin' at one another. That would be somethin' to behold. Folks would come from miles around to see somethin' like that."

He crossed the street and started toward the hotel, when he heard a woman's voice call out to him.

"Señor! Look out!"

Almost on top of the warning, Slocum felt a blow to the side of his head. He saw stars, but even as he was being hit he was reacting to the warning, so though it didn't prevent the attack, it did prevent him from being knocked down.

When his attacker swung at him a second time, Slocum was able to avoid him. With his fists up, Slocum danced quickly out to the middle of the street, avoiding any more surprises from the shadows. It wasn't until then that he saw his attacker, a large man with heavy brows and a bulbous nose.

"Mister," the man said with a low growl. "One of them men you killed back on the train was my brother and I aim to settle accounts for him."

"Fight!" someone shouted. "They's a fight in the street!"

Almost instantly, it seemed, a crowd was gathered

around Slocum and the man who had come at him out of the shadows.

"It's Frank Mason, Pete's brother," someone said.

"I'm sorry about your brother," Slocum said. "But he was trying to kill me and I didn't have any choice."

"Yeah, you had a choice," Mason said. "You could'a let him kill you."

Some in the crowd laughed nervously.

Mason swung wildly at Slocum, but Slocum slipped the punch easily, then counterpunched with a quick, slashing left to Mason's face. It was a good, well-hit blow, but Mason just flinched once, then laughed a low, evil laugh.

"Five dollars says Mason whups him," someone said.

"I don't know, I've seen men who look like this fight before. They ain't all that big, but they're tough as rawhide. I'm going with Slocum."

With an angry roar, Mason rushed Slocum again, and Slocum stepped aside, avoiding him like a matador sidestepping a charging bull. And, like a charging bull, Mason slammed into a hitching rail, smashing through it as if it were kindling. He turned and faced Slocum again.

A hush fell over the crowd now, as they watched the two men. They were watching the fight with a great deal of interest. They knew it would be a test of quickness and ability against brute strength, and they wanted to see if Slocum could handle Mason. Slocum and Mason circled around for a moment, holding their fists doubled in front of them, each trying to test the mettle of the other.

Mason swung, a clublike swing that Slocum leaned away from. Slocum counterpunched and again he scored well, but again, Mason laughed it off. As the fight went on, it developed that Slocum could hit Mason at will, and though Mason laughed off his early blows, it was soon obvious that there was a cumulative effect to Slocum's punches. Both of Mason's eyes began to puff up, and there was a nasty cut on his lip. Then Slocum caught

Mason in the nose with a long left, and when he felt the nose go under his hand, he knew that he had broken it. The bridge of his nose exploded like a smashed tomato and started bleeding profusely. The blood ran across Mason's teeth and chin.

Slocum looked for another chance at the nose, but Mason started protecting it. Slocum was unable to get it again, though the fact that Mason was favoring it told Slocum that the nose was hurting him.

Except for the opening blow, Mason hadn't connected. The big man was throwing great swinging blows toward Slocum, barely missing him on a couple of occasions, but, as yet, none of them had connected.

After four or five such swinging blows, Slocum noticed that Mason was leaving a slight opening for a good right punch, if he could just slip it across his shoulder. He timed it, and on Mason's next swing, Slocum threw a solid right, straight at the place where he thought Mason's nose would be. He timed it perfectly and had the satisfaction of hearing a bellow of pain from Mason for the first time.

Mason was obviously growing more tired now, and he began charging more and swinging less. Slocum got set for one of his charges, then as Mason rushed by with his head down, Slocum stepped to one side. Like a matador thrusting his sword into the bull in a killing lunge, Slocum sent a powerful right jab to Mason's jaw. Mason went down and out.

"Get him out of here," Slocum said, and a couple of men grabbed hold of Mason's unconscious form and dragged him away. As Mason was pulled away, the crowd began to disperse.

"Did you ever think anyone could handle Frank Mason like that?" someone asked.

"Hell, look at Slocum. His hair ain't even none messed up," another said.

"Señor?" a woman called from the shadow between two buildings. "Are you unhurt?"

"Yes, Miss Arino, thanks to you," Slocum said.

The woman gasped. "You know my name?"

"You were sitting across from me on the train."

"*Sí.*"

"You recognized the men who came on the train, didn't you?"

"*Sí.* They worked for Señor Draper." She paused for a moment. "I work for Señor Draper, too," she said.

"Yes, I know."

"How do you know these things, señor?"

"Mrs. MacTavish told me."

"She is a good woman," Juanita said.

"You know the men who attacked the train did so because they wanted to capture her, don't you?"

"Why?"

"Mrs. MacTavish thinks it is because Draper wanted to hold her prisoner, to force Mr. MacTavish into doing something he didn't want to do."

"No, I do not believe this," Juanita said. "Señor Draper is a . . . a difficult man," she said. "But I do not think he is so evil that he would do such a thing."

"Maybe not," Slocum said, not wanting to argue with her. "At any rate, I want to thank you for the warning."

5

The lobby of the New Congress Hotel was well appointed with overstuffed sofas and chairs, a rose-colored carpet, and several brass spittoons. A few strategically placed lanterns provided light, if not brightness.

The lobby was quiet and empty, except for the desk clerk who sat in a chair behind the sign-in desk, reading a copy of *Harper's Weekly*. The clerk was wearing a brown three-piece suit with a white shirt, detachable collar, and bow tie. Except for a small line of hair above each ear, he was bald. He looked up as Slocum came into the hotel.

"You would be John Slocum?" the desk clerk asked, setting his paper aside as Slocum walked up to the desk.

"Yes," Slocum replied, a little surprised that the clerk knew his name.

"Mrs. MacTavish told me you would be staying with us tonight. Wonderful woman, Mrs. MacTavish." The clerk turned toward a board that was filled with keys, hanging from hooks. He took one down from one of the hooks. "Your key, sir. You are in room two-twelve. That's upstairs, first room on the right."

Slocum noticed that when the clerk took his key down, there were none left, whereas all the other hooks representing empty rooms had two keys. He commented on it.

"Mrs. MacTavish has the other keys to all the rooms on that end of the floor," the clerk explained. "They keep them permanently rented."

"I see."

"Enjoy your stay, sir," the clerk said as he returned to his *Harper's Weekly*.

Like the lobby, the hotel room was nicely furnished. More spacious than most hotel rooms, this one had a bed, a settee, a chest of drawers, a chifforobe, and a dry sink. A porcelain pitcher and bowl sat on the dry sink.

Slocum poured water into the bowl, took off his shirt, washed, then turned the covers down to crawl into bed. It had been several weeks since he slept in a real bed and this one felt particularly comfortable.

He was awakened by a small clicking sound. Instantly his hand went to the pistol, hanging from the bed headboard. He slipped out of bed and walked barefoot across the carpet, then stood with his back to the wall just beside the door.

The click he had heard was the latch being unlocked. Now the doorknob turned. Holding his pistol in his right hand, arm crooked at the elbow, and pistol pointing up, he eased back on the hammer, cocking it so slowly that there was practically no sound as the sear engaged the cylinder.

The door opened, moving silently on the hinges. A little bar of light splashed into the room from the lighted hallway, growing larger as the door opened farther until finally it was a pie-shaped wedge that stretched from the open door all the way to the bed. Every muscle in Slocum's body tensed as he waited for the confrontation.

"John?" a woman's voice called, quietly. "John, are you in here?"

It was Julie! What was she doing in here? With a sigh, Slocum's tension was relieved, and he eased the hammer back down and lowered his pistol.

"I'm here," he said from the darkness behind her.

"Oh!" Julie said, startled by the sound from an unexpected direction. She jumped and put her hand to her chest. "Don't do that! You could scare a body to death, that way."

Slocum chuckled. "*I* could scare a body to death? What do you mean coming in my room in the middle of the night like that? I could've shot you."

"But you didn't," Julie said. In the ambient light, he could see her smile.

"No, I didn't. What are you doing in here?"

"I, uh, just wanted to see if you were all right," Julie said, lamely.

"Uh-huh. Dressed like that?"

Julie was wearing a silk nightgown that clung to her body like a second skin. It painted itself onto every curve of her body and caused her nipples to stand out in bold relief. Slocum could even see the mound between her legs.

"I didn't think you would be in here, so I didn't bother to get dressed," Julie said.

Slocum pushed the door to. "How many more keys to this door are there?" he asked.

"No more keys," Julie assured him. "I have one, you have the other." She held up her key to show and he took it from her, slipped it into the keyhole, then turned the latch. The locking bar clicked as it snapped into place.

"Now, no one will disturb us," Slocum said. He walked over to his bedside table and lit the lantern, filling the room with a soft, golden bubble of light.

"Why on earth would anyone want to distur—" That

was as far as Julie got before Slocum moved to her and
pulled her to him. He pulled her body hard against his,
kissed her, then opened his mouth as he felt her tongue
probing against his lips. He felt the heat of her body trans-
ferring itself to his as she ground her pelvis against his
huge erection.

"There is too much cloth between us," Julie said, and
she backed away from him, then pulled the silk nightgown
up and over her head. By the time she was standing nude
before him, Slocum, too, was naked, the skin of their bodies glowing softly in the splash of candlelight.

"I know you must consider me a brazen hussy," Julie
said, "coming into your room like this."

Slocum reached toward her firm, small, but well-
formed breasts. "I can't think of any way I would rather
have you come into my room," he said. Leaning down,
he brushed his lips across the nipples, moving from one
to the other.

Julie's body twitched, and Slocum felt her muscles
tighten. She brought her hands up to the sides of his head
and guided him from one breast to the other. Then, even
as he was sucking her nipples, she reached down and
wrapped her hand around his swelling shaft.

"Oh, my," she breathed as she squeezed his cock. "You
are, uh, very much a man."

Slocum picked her up and carried her over to the bed,
but when he put her on her back, she shook her head and
sat up again.

"No," she said.

"I thought you wanted to do this," Slocum started, surprised by her resistance to the move.

"I do," she said. "But not yet. Not until we've had a
little fun first."

"I was having fun," Slocum said. "I mean, I couldn't
ask for more . . . oh . . . oh, yes, I see what you mean," he
said.

The change in his tone was brought about by Julie dropping her head to take his cock into her mouth. He put his hands on the back of her head, running his fingers through her hair as she began using her mouth, working her jaws in and out, decreasing and increasing the pressure by sucking, and, most stimulating of all, by using her tongue to flick, caress, and tease him, sticking it into the little opening to bring him close.

"No," he finally said in a rasping voice. "I don't want to finish this way."

"Who said anything about being finished?" Julie replied. "Surely you are man enough to come more than once?" She returned her mouth to the task at hand and, this time, Slocum let himself go, thrusting his hips up so that he practically buried his cock in her mouth. He felt himself coming, gushing as the muscles twitched and jerked from the middle of his back, the bottom of his feet, deep in his balls, and finally ejecting in several, sensory-laden gushes. Julie stayed with him until he was completely spent.

When it was over, she moved up to lay beside him, resting her head on his shoulder.

"You didn't let me do anything for you," he said.

"You will. Just be patient," Julie said. She let her hand rest on his now flaccid cock.

"I must admit, I was very surprised to see you in here tonight," Slocum said. "From the way you were talking in the train car, I was pretty sure you'd as soon shoot me as look at me."

Julie chuckled. "I'll confess something to you," she said. "When you stopped the train and I looked out the window at you, I got all tingly and a little moist. If you had been an outlaw, coming to have your way with me, I would have been an easy target."

Slocum laughed. "That's not the way you acted when I came into the car later."

"Can you blame me? You had just threatened to shoot my aunt Emma. But later, when she explained that you had actually saved her, I understood. And, from the time I was pouring your whiskey until now, I've been planning this."

"Well, I'm glad you are a woman who follows through with her plans."

"Are you now? Hmm, and what do we have here?" she asked, squeezing his cock. "Why, John Slocum, I do believe you are getting your strength back. I'll just help it along."

Again, Julie began sucking Slocum's shaft, only this time, as he felt the pressure building up inside, he pulled himself out, then laid her on the bed and climbed on top of her. He let her guide him into her, driving deep inside her moist cunt with one, long thrust.

"Oh, yes!" Julie said. "It's wonderful! Wonderful!"

Slocum began stroking slowly with long, invading thrusts, holding himself just for a moment at the point of his deepest penetration before pulling himself out and pushing it in again.

Julie clamped her legs around his hips and clung to him as he rose and fell, and each time he reached the bottom she cried out little moans of ecstasy.

Slocum continued with her, maintaining a steady pace, timing himself by listening to her moans and feeling the reaction from her body. Taking his cue from her, he began gradually speeding up the tempo until they were no longer long, slow, deliberate strokes but hard, quick, pistonlike drives that changed her moans to short, sharp cries that she attempted to bury in his neck to keep from being overheard.

"Oh, yes, yes, yes," she was crying. "Oh, I want it. I want you! Yes, John, yes!"

Her words ran together into a sound that burst from her throat in one long, keening sob. As she cried out, she writhed and moaned, keeping her eyes shut while she shuddered in spasms of ecstasy.

Slocum, recognizing the urgency of her tone and the intensity in her movement, pounded against her with the full force of his body, driving on lustily, racing to his own climax, catching up with her as the final, smothered screams rose up from her trembling throat. He reached his peak, then fell forward on her soft, warm body as he squirted and drained himself into her, letting his muscles go limp while her final throaty sighs of satisfaction sounded softly in her ears.

Seth Draper looked at the letter Caulder had taken from the two men he had killed. It was from Cedric Nash, one of the largest and wealthiest cattlemen in the country. Cross Pass and Crown Ranch put together would make but a small corner of his landholdings. His personal wealth, it was said, rivaled the gross national product of some small nations.

"Dear Mr. MacTavish," the letter read. *"It is my understanding that some of the smaller ranchers who are your neighbors are looking for investment capital to enable them to withstand the economic pressure being put on them by an aggressive landholder.*

"It so happens that I am looking for investment opportunities and I would love to help a fellow Brit (albeit you are Scottish and I am English), give this troublesome fellow his comeuppance. I believe we can work together. Although the two young men carrying this letter, William Coleman and Darrel Scarns, are Texans, born and raised in this wonderful state, they are, in fact, my grandsons and ultimate heirs. Don't let their Texas mannerisms fool you. They are empowered to speak for me and I will honor any deal they make with you.

"Looking forward to hearing from you at the earliest, I remain, Yours Sincerely, Sir Cedric Nash."

"Grandsons?" Draper said. "Those two men were his grandsons?"

"I had no way of knowing that, Mr. Draper," Caulder said. "The way they was talking and acting, I didn't think they was nothin' but a couple of cowhands."

"Grandsons," Draper said again. He got up from the table and walked over to look through the window out onto his ranch. It was night, but the moon was shining brightly, and the vista before his eyes—gently rolling hills of silver and shadow, for as far as he could see—belonged to him. "Cedric Nash could make a great deal of trouble for us if he wanted to. He could afford to hire a private army."

"Yes, sir," Caulder said. He didn't know what else he could say.

"Well, it is a temporary setback, that's all. I don't intend to let it stop me."

"No, sir."

"Grandsons," he said again, still musing over the two young men Caulder had shot down in the Red Bull Saloon.

"I'm sorry," Caulder said. "Like I said, I didn't know."

Draper, who was a short, swarthy man with a Vandyke beard, pulled at the whiskers on his chin.

"Well, there is nothing we can do about that now," he said. "We'll just have to move up our timetable. Once we have control of everything, we will be untouchable, even by someone as big as Cedric Nash."

"What do we do next?"

"You say Mrs. MacTavish is spending the night in town?"

"Yes, sir. She and her granddaughter are at the New Congress Hotel."

Draper smiled. "Good," he said. "That presents us with a perfect opportunity."

6

A slight morning breeze filled the muslin curtains and lifted them out over the wide-planked floor. Slocum moved to the window and looked out over the town, which was just beginning to awaken. Water was being heated behind the laundry and boxes were being stacked behind the grocery store. A team of four big horses pulled a fully loaded freight wagon down the main street.

From somewhere, Slocum could smell bacon frying and his stomach growled, reminding him that he was hungry. He splashed some water in the basin, washed his face and hands, then put on his hat and went downstairs. There were a couple of people in the lobby, one napping in one of the chairs, the other reading a newspaper. Neither of them paid any attention to Slocum as he left the hotel.

The morning sun was bright, but not yet hot. The sky was clear and the air was crisp. As he walked toward the café he heard sounds of commerce: the ring of a blacksmith's hammer, a carpenter's saw, and the rattle of working wagons. That was as opposed to last night's sounds of liquor bottles, off-key piano, laughter, and boisterous conversations. How different the tenor of a town was between the business of morning and the play of evening.

Half an hour later, Slocum was enjoying a breakfast of bacon, eggs, fried potatoes, and biscuits and gravy when a boy of about sixteen came to his table.

"Excuse me," the boy said. "Are you John Slocum?"

"Yeah," Slocum replied.

"My name is Timmy Norton, Mr. Slocum. I have your horse outside."

"My horse? I don't have a horse."

"Yes, sir, you do," Timmy said. "Fact is, you got about the best horse in town. You want to see it?"

Grabbing his hat, Slocum left half a biscuit and gravy on his plate and followed Timmy outside. Standing at the hitching rail was as fine a looking example of horseflesh as he had ever seen. His saddle was on the horse.

"Where'd this horse come from?" Slocum asked.

"From Heckemeyer's," Timmy said.

"I beg your pardon?"

"Heckemeyer's. It's a stock auction barn. I work for Mr. Heckemeyer."

"All right, it came from Heckemeyer's. What I want to know is, why are you bringing it to me?"

"Oh, I thought you knew. Mrs. MacTavish bought him for you. She come by this morning and told Mr. Heckemeyer she wanted the best horse he had. He told her it would be three hundred dollars and she took it without blinking an eye. 'I'll buy it. Please see to it that Mr. John Slocum takes delivery of the animal,' she said, and that's what I'm doing here. I'm seeing to it that you take delivery."

"How'd my saddle get on him?" Slocum asked.

The boy smiled. "Heck, mister, you think I didn't figure out who you were? The whole town knows who you are and what you done on the train last night. That's purt' nigh the only thing anyone is talking about this morning.

So, I just went down there, got it, and put it on this here horse for you."

"Thanks," Slocum said.

"Say, mister?" Timmy asked. "Iffen it was to come to it, do you think you could take the Widow Maker?"

"I don't know," Slocum replied. "I've never had to try."

"Well, I know that," Timmy replied. "Iffen you had, one of you would be dead. But the question I'm askin' is, which one?"

"The one that loses," Slocum replied.

Timmy laughed. "Yeah, I reckon that's true." He looked around to make certain no one overheard him and then he said, "Well, I wouldn't mind seeing Caulder lose, that's for sure."

"You don't like your sheriff?"

"No, sir, I can't say as I do. I think he is an evil man. Besides which, he works for Seth Draper. And since I don' like Draper, I just naturally don' like anyone who works for him."

"What do you mean he works for Draper? I thought he was the town sheriff."

"He's the town sheriff because Draper made him the town sheriff," Timmy said. "That makes Caulder beholden to him."

"From what I've been able to gather, Draper is a pretty big man in these parts. I figure just about everyone is beholden to him in one way or another."

"No sir, not everyone," Timmy answered. "You know, Mr. Slocum, I didn't always work for Mr. Heckemeyer. Time was when my pa and ma and me run a ranch. It wasn't a very big ranch, but since Pa and me didn't have no hands, it was just the right size for us to run alone. But that's all gone now. Draper stole the ranch from us. My pa, he got so upset he died of the apoplexy, and my ma died of a heart that was broke. No, sir, I ain't beholden to Seth Draper at all. So if you ever do go up against the

Widow Maker, I hope I'm around to watch. And when it's all over, I hope you're the one still standin'. Be seein' you again sometime," he said.

Slocum thought about taking the horse back to Emma MacTavish. But after thinking about it for a while, he decided he would keep it. It was a good-looking horse, he needed one, and this was obviously something she wanted to do. So why not let her do it?

Slocum rode his new horse down to the sheriff's office. It had an easy gait and he could feel its power, as if it wanted to run. When he tied it at the hitching rail in front of the sheriff's office, it didn't fight the restriction.

As Caulder had warned, he wasn't in the office, but his deputy was. The deputy was rawhide thin, with a handlebar moustache and hair that hung to his shoulders. The deputy was drinking coffee, leaning back in his chair with his feet propped up on the desk.

"You would be Percy?" Slocum asked.

The deputy grinned, showing stained, crooked teeth. "Yeah. You've heard of me?"

"I got your name from Caulder. You get any word back from the capital on those men I shot?"

"Yeah, Caulder told me about you," Percy said. "We've checked, Slocum. There ain't no reward."

"What about up in Colorado? Kansas? Texas? You check with them?"

"No, and I didn't check China, either," Percy answered. "I told you, there ain't no dodgers out on these men. These men worked for Mr. Draper. As a matter of fact, if I was you, I'd be leavin' town about now. Mr. Draper don't take too kind to folks who kill his men."

"And does that include you, Deputy? Are you one of Draper's men?"

"Like Sheriff Caulder, Deputy Boyle is bought and paid for," a woman's voice said, and Slocum turned to see Emma MacTavish standing in the door.

"Look here, Mrs. MacTavish, you got no right to say something like that," Percy said.

"Of course I do. It's called the truth," Emma said.

"What do you want?" Percy asked.

"I came to find out if the sheriff has made any progress in finding out who is rustling our cattle."

"The sheriff ain't here," Percy said. "But I can tell you that we are working on it."

"Working on it," Emma replied with derision. "I'll just bet you are. Why don't you go out to Crown Ranch and examine some of his cattle. I think you'll find that many more than a few brands have been changed."

"Be reasonable, Mrs. MacTavish," Percy said. "You just got accusations, you got no proof. We can't go charging out onto Crown Ranch making all these accusations without proof."

"You and Caulder wouldn't charge onto Crown Ranch with all the proof in the world and with the United States Army marching along beside you."

Emma turned away angrily, then swept back down the street toward the depot and her private car. Percy stood in the window watching her for a moment, then he turned back to Slocum.

"Who the hell does she think she is?" the deputy asked. "Ridin' around in that fancy railcar, tryin' to tell me how to do my job. She's tryin' to fool people into thinkin' she's some great lady or somethin'. Well, I could tell you a few stories about her, if you'd like to know."

"I don't want to hear any of them," Slocum said. "The lady is my friend."

"Your friend, huh? Well, it's too bad you didn't run into her some years back. From what I hear she was *real* friendly with men then, if you know what I mean. They say there was a time when . . . arhhhg!" The deputy's tale was interrupted by the barrel of a pistol, shoved into his throat. His eyes grew wide with fright and he looked at Slocum in terror and confusion.

"I said I didn't want to hear any of the stories," Slocum said quietly. "Do I make myself clear now?"

To the degree the deputy could respond with a pistol barrel shoved halfway down his throat, Percy nodded yes. Slocum took the gun out of the deputy's mouth, wiped the barrel on Percy's pants leg, then put it away.

"What's the matter with you? Are you crazy?" the deputy asked.

"Just crazy enough to give me an edge," Slocum said. He twisted his mouth into what might have been a smile. "This way nobody ever knows just what I'm going to do."

"Somebody could get hurt, you doin' something like that," the deputy complained, taking his handkerchief out to wipe his mouth. The blade sight of Slocum's pistol had cut Percy's lip and he pulled the handkerchief away to examine the blood. There wasn't much.

"Generally somebody does get hurt," Slocum replied easily. "And lots of times they get killed. Only it isn't me."

After Slocum left the sheriff's office, he got a bath and a haircut at the barbershop, then changed into his clean shirt and pants while he took the ones he was wearing to the laundry. He bought some fresh bullets for his gun, as well as some coffee, beans, and jerky. He waited until his laundry was done, then he picked it up and started to ride out of town.

He had a notion to go on. He didn't need to get mixed up in all the goings-on in Prosperity. The fact that Julie had come into his room last night had been great, but also dangerous. She was too nice a girl, and too vulnerable. He knew that there was no chance for any kind of a real relationship between them; she was the granddaughter of a very powerful and wealthy family, he was a drifter.

Eventually he would ride on, and when he did, she would be hurt.

He also had to think about Caulder, the man they called the Widow Maker. There was already bad blood between them. Well, not between them, actually, Caulder didn't remember Slocum and probably couldn't even remember the two men he had killed. Slocum remembered them though, and he knew it would take very little provocation for him to give everyone in town what they were wanting to see. A gunfight between John Slocum and James Caulder.

As he approached the railcar though, he knew he wouldn't be able to leave without at least saying good-bye. Also, he owed Mrs. MacTavish thanks for the horse. He tugged on the reins, then guided the horse over to the sidetrack.

Slocum pulled his hand back to knock on the door but it was jerked open before he could do so. Julie greeted him with a smile.

"I was hoping you would stop by," she said. "Please come in, Manuel is preparing lunch for us."

"Manuel?"

"He used to cook for us out at the ranch," Emma explained, coming over to greet Slocum as well. "But when he got married, he left us and started his own restaurant here in town. He still cooks for us on special occasions though, and I asked him to come over and prepare lunch for us today."

"Really, I didn't plan to eat, I just wanted . . ." Slocum interrupted in midsentence. "What is that wonderful smell?"

"You like it?" Emma said, smiling. "It is a special recipe Manuel has come up with, using marinated beef, cumin, and green chilis. He calls it *Alimento de los Dioses*. Food of the Gods."

"I reckon I'll stay," Slocum said.

"I thought you might."

"By the way, I want to thank you for the horse."

"Thank Julie. She was the one who pointed out to me that the only reason we met you in the first place was because you had lost your horse. She wanted to show you our appreciation for what you did for us last night."

Slocum looked over at Julie. How different she looked now, cool, composed, and as detached as if last night never happened. He could almost believe he had dreamed it, but he knew he hadn't.

"I thought you showed me that last night, in the hotel room," he said, speaking directly to Julie.

His comment had the desired effect, for she actually blushed, then looked over at her aunt Emma.

"I beg your pardon?" Emma asked. "How did she do that?"

"I meant both of you," Slocum said easily. "By providing me with a hotel room."

"Oh," Emma said.

Julie breathed a bit easier, then smiled at Slocum, as if telling him that she appreciated their private joke.

"Do you like the horse?" Emma asked.

"Yes, I do. It's a great horse."

"What have you named him?"

"Horse, I guess," Slocum said. "He's a tool, not a pet."

Emma laughed. "You are a practical man, aren't you, John Slocum?"

"Most of the time."

Manuel served their meal then. Slocum had eaten many Mexican meals in his life, including more than his share in Mexico. Most of them consisted of tortillas and beans, or maybe a taco with spicy beef. None of them had ever been like this one. This was one of the most delicious meals he had ever eaten and he told that to a beaming Manuel.

Just as they were finishing their meal, Slocum heard someone calling Emma from outside.

"Mrs. MacTavish! Mrs. MacTavish!" The shouts were accompanied by the staccato sound of hoofbeats from a galloping horse.

Julie got up from the table and peered through the curtains. "Aunt Emma, it's Dan," she said.

"Dan? What's he doing here?" Emma also got up from the table but instead of looking through the window, she stepped out onto the back of the car. Julie and Slocum followed.

Dan rode all the way up to the car at a gallop, then swung down from his horse. The animal was lathered from exertion and Dan was out of breath.

"Dan, look at that poor animal. You have nearly killed it," Emma scolded. "What on earth possesses you to do such a thing?"

"It's Mr. MacTavish," Dan said.

Emma gasped and put her hand to her chest. "Ian? What? What has happened?"

"He's gone, Mrs. MacTavish," Dan said.

"Gone? What do you mean gone? Good heavens! You don't mean he has died?"

"No, ma'am. Leastwise, I don't think so," Dan said. "But last night, in the middle of the night, some riders come out to the ranch and well, they . . . they . . ."

"They what, man? Speak up!"

"They took him."

"Took him?"

"Yes, ma'am. At gunpoint. They just kicked open the door of the house, went inside, and took him."

"And nobody did anything?"

"We couldn't do anything, Mrs. MacTavish," Dan explained. "We was all asleep in the bunkhouse and didn't know nothin' about it till it was too late. When we heard Mr. MacTavish yellin', we all run out front to see what was goin' on. When we did, we found ourselves lookin' down the barrels of half a dozen guns. The ones that wasn't takin' Mr. MacTavish was all gathered around the front of the bunkhouse just waitin' on us. There we was, standin' out front in our underwear, and there they was, sitting on their horses, holdin' their guns pointed at us."

"Did you recognize any of them?" Emma asked.

"Well, they was all wearin' hoods over their heads so's we couldn't recognize 'em," Dan said. "But I'm sure one of 'em was Bodine. You 'member him, don't you, Mrs. MacTavish. Mr. MacTavish fired him last year."

"I remember him," Julie said. "He went to work for Draper, didn't he?"

"Yes'm, he did."

Because of the way Dan had galloped into town, several of the town's citizens had come down to the rail siding to see what was going on. Others, seeing the gathering crowd, joined them to satisfy their own curiosity so that soon a rather substantial group of people were standing around the car, listening to the conversation. The crowd of people brought the deputy down as well, not because he thought there might be some official function to perform, but because he was as curious as the others.

Seeing Percy in the crowd, Emma called out to him.

"So, what are you going to do now, Deputy Boyle? Draper has quit stealing cows and has stolen my husband."

"We don't know that," Percy said.

"Of course we know it," Julie said in exasperation. "You heard Dan say that one of the men who came in the middle of the night was Bodine."

"Yes'm, I heard him say he thinks Bodine was one of the men. But he also said they was all wearin' hoods, so if they was, how can he be sure? And even if it was Bodine, that don't prove that Draper had anything to do with it."

"Percy, you are either an idiot or a coward," Emma said harshly. "Never mind, I'll take care of it."

Percy pointed a long, bony finger at Emma. "Now, Mrs. MacTavish, as a deputy sheriff, I'm warnin' you, don't you go takin' things into your own hands. You wait until Sheriff Caulder gets back. Let him handle this."

"Handle it?" Emma said, angrily. "That son of a bitch probably led the men who did this."

"I'm warning you," Percy said again, but when he saw Slocum staring hard at him, he withered under the stare, then turned and went back to his office.

"Come inside, Dan," Emma invited. "Catch your breath, and have something to eat."

"Yes, ma'am," Dan said, gratefully.

Emma, Julie, Slocum, and Dan went back into the car, and with the initial excitement over, the crowd dispersed.

"John, when your horse went down yesterday, where were you headed?" Emma asked.

"Nowhere in particular," Slocum admitted.

"Uh-huh, I thought as much. I'd like to talk a little business with you."

"What kind of business?"

"I want you to go out to Crown Ranch, find my husband, and bring him home. If you do that for me, I will give you fifteen hundred dollars."

Slocum whistled. "That's a lot of money."

"Aunt Emma, you can't send one man out to do something like that," Julie said. "You'll get him killed."

"Ian is going to be killed if we don't get him out of there," Emma said. "Besides, I wasn't planning on sending him alone. We've got more than two dozen hands out at the ranch. I'm sure I can find several who will ride with John."

"You can count me in," Dan said.

"You any good with a gun?" Slocum asked.

"Well, I've never had to use one 'ceptin' against snakes

and such," Dan said. "But I don't reckon there's much a fella would have to learn."

"Anyone else out at Cross Pass good with a gun?"

Dan shook his head. "They're all about like me."

Slocum looked up at Emma. "Sorry, Mrs. MacTavish, but if you put together a bunch of riders from your ranch, you'll like as not get about half of them killed."

"We'll take that chance," Dan said, resolutely.

"I won't. I might be one of them in that half. I'm uncomfortable around an army that doesn't know what it's doing."

"Then you won't do it?"

"I didn't say I wouldn't do it," Slocum said. "I just don't want to do it with a bunch of amateurs."

Emma grinned broadly, then poured Slocum a glass of the sipping whiskey he had enjoyed the night before.

"You're sure Mr. MacTavish is out at Crown Ranch?"

"I have no proof," Emma said. "If you need proof, I'm sorry, I can't furnish that."

Slocum laughed. "Mrs. MacTavish, I don't try people in a court of law. To my way of looking at things, there are only two sides to the coin. True, or not true. If it is true that Draper has your husband, then I don't give a damn about proof."

Emma smiled broadly. "I knew we were going to be able to work together," she said.

7

"I have a map that might help," Emma said. She was just reaching for it when there was a knock on the door of the car. Slocum put his hand on his pistol but when Julie looked through the window, she breathed a sigh of relief. "It's alright, it's just Lane," she said.

"Lane?"

"Clint Lane. He used to be the sheriff," Emma said. "Until Draper paid off the town council and had him replaced with Caulder."

"He's a good man," Dan said.

"Let him in, dear," she added to Julie.

Clint Lane was a man in his late thirties to early forties. There was a solid look about him, the look of someone who is dependable and trustworthy, but Slocum didn't see the hard edge a man might need to go up against someone like Seth Draper, and certainly not to confront James Caulder.

"Hello, Mrs. MacTavish, Julie, Dan," Lane said. He looked at Slocum.

"Clint, this is John Slocum," Emma said, introducing him.

"Yeah, I know who he is," Lane said. "You're the one who killed those men on the train, aren't you?"

"I am."

"Is it true that you also threatened to shoot Mrs. MacTavish?"

"It wasn't like that, Clint. He was running a bluff on the gunman who was holding a gun on me."

"By threatening to shoot you?" Lane asked. It was clear he didn't approve of the tactic.

"Believe me, it was the only way," Emma insisted. "Do you think I would let him in here if I thought he really was going to shoot me?"

"Clint, he saved Aunt Emma's life," Julie said.

The expression on Lane's face softened, then he smiled and extended his hand. "Well, if you are all right with these ladies, you are all right with me," he said. He turned his attention to Dan.

"I heard some night riders took Ian MacTavish."

"That's right."

"You mean they came right onto the ranch, took him, and there was nothing you nor the other hands could do?"

"We've been through that, Clint," Emma said. "It was the middle of the night and the boys were all asleep in the bunkhouse. When they heard the commotion and went outside to see what was going on, there were armed men waiting for them."

"You think we would've let him be taken if we could have prevented it?" Dan asked.

"I guess not. Is it true that Bodine was one of them?"

"Yeah," Dan said. "They were all wearing hoods, but one of them was Bodine, I'd swear to it."

"Bodine is riding for Crown Ranch now, isn't he?"

"Yes," Dan said. "I fired him off Cross Pass. Well, wasn't my job to fire or hire, but I recommended to Mr. MacTavish that they fire him. He was a thief, a bully, and a troublemaker. He had no place working with decent men."

"So he went to work for Crown Ranch where he would be amongst his own kind," Emma said.

"Yes, well, Draper's not going to get away with it this time," Lane said. "I'm going to ride up to the capital and tell the territorial governor what's going on down here. I think it's time we got a federal marshal down here."

"By the time you got back it would be too late," Slocum said.

"The truth of the matter is, I should've gone up there long before now, but I had no idea it would go this far," Lane said. "Also, having just lost my job, I was afraid that going to the territorial governor to complain might look like sour grapes. I don't know, maybe it is too late, but we've got to do something."

"We are going to do something," Emma said.

"Whatever it is, count me in."

"Mr. Slocum is going out to Crown Ranch to get Ian back."

"What? You mean you are just going to ride out there and take him?"

"Something like that."

"Great!" Lane said. "You can count me in."

Slocum studied Lane for a long moment, trying to decide whether taking him along would be a help or a hindrance. He was certain that the former sheriff's intentions were good, and he believed he could trust him. But years of living on the edge had given him the unique ability to judge others, not only their character, but their potential. Clint Lane passed the character test, but failed the potential. Slocum knew that if he took him with him, Clint Lane would get killed.

"No," he said. "I work better alone."

"Are you crazy? Do you know how many men Draper has out there? He has at least twenty," Draper said, answering his own question. "Maybe more. How is one man going to go up against twenty?"

"Two men wouldn't make the odds much better," Slocum replied. "One man is more likely to slip through. Also, there's no worry about the other man. Believe me, Lane, I know what I'm doing. I've been in situations like this before."

"Yeah, I'm sure you have," Lane replied a bit caustically.

"Clint," Julie chided.

"He's right, Clint," Dan said. "Like you, I offered to go. But if you think about it, his way is better."

Clint sighed, then took off his hat and ran his hand through his hair. Slocum saw a lot of gray.

"I know I'm not the sheriff anymore, but I can't just lay down the responsibility. And I especially can't just stand by and see friends get in trouble, and not try to help."

"You're going to help."

"How?"

"I don't know yet, but I'll find a way to use you, I promise. Look, all I'm going to do now is just ride out there to have a look around," Slocum said. "I'll come up with a plan when I get back."

"All right," Lane said. "So long as you agree to let me help."

"Agreed," Slocum said. Then, he turned to Emma. "Now, what do you say we have a look at that map you were going to show me."

Emma unrolled the map on the table.

"Here is Cross Pass, up here." She pointed to a sizable piece of land. "And this is Crown Ranch."

Crown Ranch was a much larger piece.

"As you can see, for several miles, the borders of the two ranches are contiguous," Emma pointed out. "But these," she continued, "are the ranches that are causing all the trouble."

There were half a dozen smaller spreads, wedged in between Cross Pass Station and Crown Ranch.

"Trouble?"

"Well, not for us," Emma explained. "For Draper." She pointed to another part of the map. "You see, he has already bought out, or run out, the people who were working these ranches." Slocum saw that several smaller spreads had been assimilated into Crown Ranch. "He didn't have any trouble doing that because he controlled their water. The Wahite River runs across his property, and according to this map, it also feeds these ranches down here. That is, it *did* feed these ranches. But the map is deceiving, John. There *is* no Wahite River anymore."

"Why is that?"

"I'll answer that question," Lane said. "There's no Wahite River anymore, because that son of a bitch has put in a bunch of dams. He has completely stopped the river's flow. At least, beyond this point."

"Do you know where the dams are?" Slocum asked.

Lane shook his head. "No."

"I know where they are," Dan said. "I know where every one of the damn things are."

"Can you mark them on this map?"

"Sure."

After Dan marked the locations of each of the dams, Emma continued her orientation.

"All the ranches that were dependent upon the Wahite are gone," she explained. "Draper dried up the ranches and forced them out. But, look at these ranches. These are still operating, because a creek flows through each one of them. These are the ranches that are causing him trouble."

Slocum looked at the map, then followed the creek back to its source.

"The spring head is on Cross Pass Station," he said.

"Yes. And as long as we control that spring head, the smaller ranchers are assured of getting their fair share of water. Draper has been trying to buy the spring head, and if he ever gets it, he will do exactly as he did with the Wahite. Once the water is gone, the smaller ranchers will be gone as well."

"So you're protecting the smaller ranchers?"

"Yes," Emma said. "But it's not all charity. It's for self-protection, because once those ranches are gone, he'll come after us. We'll be the little rancher then."

"That's simple, don't sell."

"We have told him that we have no intention of selling," Emma said. "But he has managed to make things very difficult for us. We lost so many cattle through rustling last year that, for the first time, the ranch actually failed to turn a profit."

"Rustling?"

"Draper," Dan said. "There is no doubt that he is the one doing it. I mean I've seen some of the cows he has rebranded. It's not hard to turn a CP into a CR, but sometimes his men mess up on something even that simple."

"Have you called him on it?"

"One of the rebranded cows wandered back onto our ranch and we brought Caulder out to look at it," Emma said. "But it was a waste of time. He couldn't see, or else wouldn't see, the obvious."

"Now you can see why Draper had me replaced as sheriff," Lane said. "With his own man in office, he can do anything he wants and get away with it."

Emma ran her hand through her hair. "Well, I don't intend on letting him get away with taking Ian. Whatever it takes, I'm going to get my husband back, then I'm going to see to it that Draper pays."

"What I don't understand is why they took him," Julie said.

"I'm sure he intends to ransom him to us in exchange for our agreement to sell the spring head to him," Emma said.

"I'm afraid you are right," Slocum said.

"I'm glad you have agreed to help."

"There's one thing you need to know about me, Mrs. MacTavish," Slocum said.

"What is that?"

"People have a habit of dying around me. I guess you saw an example of that last night. I didn't set out to kill those men, but somehow it tends to build upon itself. Lots of times when people are around me, they try to kill me and I have no choice. I generally have to kill them."

"So, what are you telling me?"

"I'm telling you that if I go onto Crown Ranch to look for Mr. MacTavish, some people are going to be killed. Maybe a lot of people. Does that bother you?"

"Not if one of them isn't Ian."

"That's just the point," Slocum said. "There is no guarantee that one of them won't be Ian."

Emma brushed a fall of hair back from her face, a gesture that made her look vulnerable and much younger. She sighed. "John, I know there is a risk in this," she said. "There's a risk in everything. But I have to do something, and I would rather fight than give in to that low-life son of a bitch."

Slocum laughed. "Every man should have a woman like you, Mrs. MacTavish."

Juanita Arino, Seth Draper's maid, slept in a very small, windowless alcove at the rear of the second floor. She had been awakened in the middle of the night by strange and somewhat disconcerting sounds coming from downstairs. Getting out of bed, she put on a wrapper, then slipped quietly down the hall to the head of the stairs. From here, she could see the big clock that sat in the foyer at the foot of the stairs. It was three-thirty in the morning. Only three-thirty in the morning, but the living room was filled with people.

Why are there so many people at this hour? Then she wondered if something bad had happened, for the voices were gruff and angry.

Perhaps she should go down to the kitchen to make coffee. Whatever it was, they would probably welcome a hot cup of coffee. She started back to her room to get dressed when she heard Ian MacTavish's voice. She recognized it because her cousin, Manuel, used to work for MacTavish and she had visited Cross Pass many times. She went back to the head of the stairs, then slipped, quietly, down several of the steps, far enough to allow her to look into the living room.

MacTavish was standing there, held on either side by a couple of Draper's men. In addition to the two men who were holding MacTavish, there were three others in the room: Sheriff Caulder, Bodine, and Draper himself. Both Bodine and Caulder were holding pistols, pointed at MacTavish. Draper, who wasn't armed, was leaning against the fireplace mantel.

"Draper, have ye gone mad now?" MacTavish asked.

"I thought if we got together, we could discuss things like reasonable men," Draper replied. "That is why I decided to invite you over for a little talk."

"Invite me over is it? Sendin' these black-hearted scoundrels to steal me in the middle of the night? I'd nae be callin' that an invitation."

Draper chuckled. "It's obvious that you weren't in a very receptive mood. Look at them, black eyes, swollen lips, broken teeth. For an old man, MacTavish, you must've put up one hell of a fight."

"Old man, am I? I can still take you and any two of your best men," MacTavish said. "Of course, laddie, that's nae saying a whole lot, if the likes of these are your best.

Bodine? 'Tis a known fact he's as worthless as spit on a hot skillet."

"If it doesn't work out, Mr. Draper, and you decide to kill this old bastard, I want the privilege of doin' it," Bodine said. Even from the top of the stairs, Juanita could see that Bodine's face was bruised.

"So it's killin' me you want, is it, Bodine? That you'll never do. You've nae got what it takes to kill a Mac-Tavish."

"Think not? We'll just see about that, you son of a bitch! I'll just kill you right now!" Bodine cocked his pistol.

"Bodine, hold it!" Draper warned. "If you kill him, I'll kill you."

All the talk of killing made Juanita's blood run cold, and she crossed herself. This was even more frightening than the events that happened on the train last night. Then, four men had been killed, but it had happened so quickly and spontaneously that Juanita didn't have time to be afraid. Here, men were talking about killing each other. It was the cold-blooded premeditation that made it so chilling.

"I won't kill him yet," Bodine said, lowering the hammer on his pistol. "But I can hardly wait until you say it's all right."

"What do you want to do with him?" Caulder asked.

"For now, take him up to the attic," Draper said. "We'll keep him up there until his wife gives me what I want."

"You think she'll come around?"

"She will if she ever wants to see him alive again," Draper said.

So interested was she in what was going on that when they started bringing MacTavish up the stairs, she almost got caught. Gasping, she moved quickly back down the hallway then stood in the shadows at the far end as she saw them pull down the trapdoor and lower the ladder that led to the attic.

So, it was true, what everyone was saying about Draper. She had told Slocum that she didn't believe he intended to make Señora MacTavish his hostage, but now, she had to face the fact that it was true. He really had intended to take her and, unable to do so, had taken Señor MacTavish instead.

"What's Draper going to do with him?" Juanita heard one of the men ask.

"He's going to keep him until he gets what he wants, then he's going to kill him."

"Good enough for the bastard, him and his uppity foreign ways."

Juanita slipped back into her alcove and said a prayer for poor Señor MacTavish.

8

After Slocum left, Emma poured herself a glass of what Ian called "morning mist, bottled right from the Scottish moors."

In a lot of ways, Slocum reminded her of Ian when he was younger. They had the same self-confidence, aggressive spirit, and take-charge attitude. She also thought, warming with the remembrance, that they had the same raw sex appeal.

It was thirty years ago when Ian MacTavish walked through the door of the Lucky Nugget Saloon in San Francisco. He was a powerfully built man with a red beard, ruddy complexion, and flashing blue eyes.

He was also wearing a kilt, complete with belt and elaborate buckle, sash, broach, short knife, and leather pouch. His costume elicited a great deal of derisive laughter from the others in the saloon.

"Hey, Red," one of the men called. "Where'd you get that dress?"

"Sure, laddie, and you're nae makin' fun o' my kilt now, are ye?"

"Your what?"

"My kilt," Ian explained patiently. "In my country, 'tis the dress of a gentleman. Of course, you nae being a gentleman, you would know nothing of that."

"Maybe I ain't a gentleman, but I sure ain't no girly-boy," the detractor said, and his comment was met with more laughter.

"Oh, laddie, do nae be tellin' me now that 'tis less than a man you're callin' me. Sure'n that would get my dander up," Ian said.

"You mean that would make you mad? Oh, don't get mad at me, girly-boy. I would be really afraid." He shuddered pointedly.

"You have gone and done it, haven't you? You've nae sense o' respect for the MacTavish tartan."

"What you got under that there dress, anyhow?" the detractor asked, coming toward him. "Hell, I bet you ain't even got a cock under there."

"Sure'n would you like to lift it up and have yourself a wee bit of a look?" Ian invited.

With the smile spread across his face, Ian's tormentor walked over to him. Holding his drink in one hand, he reached down to grab the hem of Ian's kilt with the other. When he did, Ian hit him with an uppercut blow from his right hand, so powerful that it lifted him bodily from the floor and deposited him on a table several feet away. He fell on the table, breaking it in two with his weight.

"Hey, what the hell? That's my friend!" one of the other bar patrons said, and he charged at Ian, but Ian took him down with one blow as well. At least three others tried attacking Ian, all at the same time, but he was a whirling dervish of speed and power. In less than two minutes, Ian MacTavish had taken the best of five men.

" 'Tis thankful to you laddies I am for providin' Ian MacTavish with a wee bit o' fun," Ian said. "Will there nae be another to join in the game?"

When he got no answer he beat himself on the chest and let out a load roar. "I'm Ian MacTavish, chief o' the MacTavish clan, and I'll take the measure o' anyone who tries me!"

It was clear by then that no one else wanted to test his claim as the others moved away, nursing their drinks and doing all they could to avoid eye contact with the red-haired, red-bearded giant.

"In that case," Ian said, the frown being replaced by a broad smile, "I can nae see a reason we can nae all be friends." He looked at the men who were lying around in various positions on the floor, having been put there by his fists. "Here lads, let me help you up," he offered. Reaching down a big hand he jerked them onto their feet, one by one, picking them up as easily as if they were children. "Barkeep?"

"Yes, sir?" the bartender replied cautiously.

From the purse he wore strapped to him, MacTavish took a large amount of money and slapped it on the bar. "Would you be for providin' these lads and lassies with a wee bit o' the creature?" he said.

"How much of the, uh, creature?"

"Oh, lad, sure'n they can all drink till the money is gone," MacTavish said. "And be for takin' yourself a generous tip."

"Yes, sir!" the bartender replied enthusiastically, his eyes growing large at the amount of money Ian showed him.

"Laddies, step up to the bar and enjoy yourselves on Ian MacTavish," Ian said. Then, turning toward the women who had been looking on in awe, his smile broadened. "I intend to choose myself a lassie and have myself some sport."

Ian didn't hesitate. He went directly to Emma Ritter. She was surprised by that. Though she wasn't the youngest of the soiled doves who were working the bar, she was the newest to the profession, having taken up the trade when her husband died less than a month earlier.

"Would you be for comin' upstairs with me now, lass?" Ian asked, reaching out to take her hand.

In her short time in the business, Emma had already been with several men. Nearly all of the men treated the girls with respect. That was because the ratio of men to women was roughly four hundred to one and whores were much more than a vice, they were practically a necessity. As a result, Emma had never had a really bad experience, but neither had she ever felt anything like the transference of energy she felt when Ian touched her. She led him upstairs to her room, unable to understand why she was tingling inside at the thought of what was to come.

"This is my room," she said, leading him into the tiny, ten-foot-by-ten-foot cubicle. Since arriving here, she had done what she could to turn the room into a home. A sampler on the wall read, "God bless this home." The window had curtains, and the bed was covered with a brightly colored patchwork quilt. There were fresh wild-flowers in a vase on the dry sink.

"You can tell much about a person by lookin' at the way they live," Ian said. "What's your name, lassie?"

"Emma." Emma started to tell him her last name but decided against it. Telling him her husband's name just before going to bed with him made it seem like she was cheating on her husband. It's funny, she had never felt that way with anyone else. But she had never really looked forward to it with anyone else.

" 'Tis a pretty name, Emma."

"Thank you." She looked at the kilt. "I've never seen one of those before."

"Have you, nae? 'Tis the native costume of my coun-try." He showed her the orange and green plaid of his kilt. "Each clan has its own tartan, you see. And when you see this design, in this color, you'll know 'tis the tartan o' the MacTavish clan."

Emma reached down to touch it, then, almost as if her hand was guided by itself, it moved down to clasp the hem of the kilt.

Ian laughed. "Is it underneath the kilt you're wantin' to see?"

"What do you wear under the kilt?"

"Well, Emma, because it's you, I'll be for lettin' you see what the ill-mannered gentleman in the bar downstairs could nae see," Ian said as he unwrapped his kilt.

"Oh, my!" Emma said, gasping. "You aren't wearing anything!"

"Not true, Emma, m'girl. I'm wearin' a hard-on, just for you."

There was no further conversation; there was no need for it. Emma undressed, feeling her body tremble as she did so. A moment later she was nude and stretched out on the bed. Ian leaned down to kiss her breasts, and the touch of his tongue to her nipples sent shudders of pleasure rippling through her.

Now Ian raised up and looked down at her body as he finished undressing. Emma felt his languid appraisal of her body without embarrassment. In fact, she took pleasure from his slow, hot gaze, tingling everywhere his glance lingered, as though he was actually touching her there.

When he got into bed with her, Ian caressed her with skillful, tender supplication. He explored her body with the easy confidence and expertise of an experienced lover. Soon a flood of passion, unlike anything she had ever experienced before, even with her late husband, swept her along until she was returning his caresses with unchecked desire. She felt her fluids literally bubbling up from between her legs and she could almost believe she was about to drown in her own juices.

Ian finally entered her and with a moan of pleasure she rose to meet him. She locked her arms around him, drawing him to her and burying her head in his neck and wrapping her legs around his torso as she took him into her.

Never before had it been like this. So, this was what the poets wrote about . . . this was what the men craved when they stood in line, one after another to share her bed.

Suddenly there was an explosion of sensation bursting within, spreading rapidly through her body in concentric waves of rapture. After that there was another, and still another, and yet another. Emma rode with the pleasures of the experience until the flaming meteor's blaze was but a glowing cinder, still warm, but no longer burning.

She couldn't hold back her cry of ecstasy.

"Aunt Emma, are you all right?" Julie asked.

"What dear?" Emma replied, being jerked back to the present.

"It sounded like you were moaning or something."

"Oh, uh, I was just thinking about your uncle, that's all."

Misunderstanding, Julie came over to her aunt and put her arms around her. "Yes, I'm worried about him too. But I just know that John will get him back for us. Maybe it's irrational of me to believe that, but, somehow I just know that he will."

"It's not irrational at all, dear. I have the same sense of confidence. And not just in Mr. Slocum, but in Ian as well. He's grown old, but don't underestimate him. He is a strong-willed man and he will do whatever it takes to survive."

"That's what Papa used to say," Julie said. "He always said that if the Devil and his brother were to go into the same room for an all-out brawl, it would be Ian Mac-Tavish who would come out victorious."

Emma laughed. "Your papa knew Ian well. It's a shame he and your mother . . ." She stopped in midsentence. "The fever was awful, but the one good thing to come out of it was that it sent you to live with us. Ian and I have had a wonderful marriage, but for some reason we never had children. Then, one day we look up, and here is the prettiest, bounciest, sweetest twelve-year-old young girl a person could ever hope for, come to be like our very own daughter."

"I remember being scared to death when I first came out here," Julie said. "I had no idea what to expect. What a wonderful experience it has been."

Aunt and niece embraced warmly, providing each other with comfort and reassurance as they waited out the fate of the man who was so dear to them both.

Ian MacTavish was chained to the bed. He was angry with himself for allowing Draper's men to come into his bedroom and capture him, trap him like he was a rabbit or something.

Of course, it hadn't been that easy for them. Even though they surprised him, he had fought back, knocking the teeth out of Bodine, nearly tearing the nose off another and turning an ear into cauliflower on the third. It was not until Bodine hit him on the head with a pistol butt, not once, but twice, that he was stunned into submission. By the time he regained his senses, his hands were chained behind his back and someone was pointing a loaded pistol at him.

The men who took him in the middle of the night were all wearing hoods, but when he saw they had brought him to Crown Ranch, he wasn't surprised. He had been here for nearly twelve hours now, and hadn't seen a soul since he arrived. He was getting hungry and he wondered if Draper was going to feed him.

Even as he thought of Draper, Draper came into the room, carrying a bowl.

"I have some stew for you, MacTavish," he said.

"Put it on the table."

"You can't say thanks?" Draper asked, setting the bowl down.

"Am I supposed to be grateful to you, you heathen bastard, for comin' to my house like a thief in the night and stealin' me away from my own kith 'n' kin?"

"I just brought you here so we could have a little talk," Draper said.

"A talk, is it?" Ian rattled the chains that held him prisoner. "And this is to make me hear you better?"

"Yes," Draper said. "Let's face it, MacTavish. You would've never come here on your own."

"You got that right."

"It doesn't have to be like this, you know," Draper continued. "We should be friends, you and I. We are the two largest landowners around, perhaps in the entire territory. Men like us should stick together against the homesteaders and claim jumpers who are all around. After all, we are just alike."

"We are nae alike, Seth Draper," Ian said with a snarl. "You are a peasant. You can have as much land and wealth as any lord in the realm but, with it all, you are still a lowlife."

"Funny that you would call me a lowlife when you are the one who married a whore," Draper said.

Ian's roar of anger caused the chickens in the barn to scatter.

9

Slocum looked back over his shoulder as he led the four horses across the swiftly running stream. Each animal was carrying a body, belly down, across his back. The bodies were well wrapped in tarpaulin, but that didn't keep the horses from smelling death and they didn't like it one little bit.

The horses were the same ones the men had been riding when they stopped the train. A freight-train crew found them the next day, calmly cropping grass alongside the track where the outlaws left them. They put the horses in an empty cattle car and brought them on into Prosperity.

Slocum didn't know which body belonged to which horse, but he didn't care. He just tossed them on, first come, first served. Caulder still wasn't back in his office, but Percy told him he was a fool to be taking the bodies out to Draper's ranch. However, he made no effort to stop him.

The horses kicked up sheets of silver spray as they trotted through the stream. Slocum would have paused to give them an opportunity to drink if they wanted to, but none of them did. It was as if they were anxious to get to where they were going so they could rid themselves of their gruesome cargo.

Once across the stream, Slocum turned back around to pay attention to where he was going. For some time now he had been aware that two men were dogging him, riding parallel with him and, for the most part, staying out of sight. He was pretty sure they were Crown Ranch men, and they were good at what they were doing. They were good, but Slocum was better. He had picked them up the moment they started shadowing him.

Slocum rode on for a couple more miles, all the while keeping his eye on them, until finally he decided to do something about it. He waited until the trail led in between two parallel rows of hills. Once into the defile, he dropped the line to the lead horse, knowing that it could only go forward, then he cut off the trail and, using the ridgeline to conceal his movement, rode ahead about two hundred yards. He went over to the gully his two tails were using, dismounted, then pulled his rifle from the saddle scabbard and climbed onto a rocky ledge to wait for them. He jacked a round into the chamber.

Slocum watched and waited. He saw them come around a bend in the gully and knew that not only had they not seen him, they hadn't even missed him. When they were right on him, he suddenly stood up.

"Hold it!" he shouted.

"Goddamn!" one of the riders yelled. He had to fight to stay on his horse, for the horse had been so startled that it reared. The other rider started for his gun.

"Don't do it!" Slocum said, raising his rifle to his shoulder.

"Buck, keep your hand away from your gun!" the first rider said, just now regaining control of his horse.

Buck stopped his draw. "Where'd you come from?" he asked.

"You ought to know," Slocum replied. "You've been dogging my tail for the last five miles."

"I don't know what you're talking about."

"Mister, don't insult my intelligence," Slocum said. "That makes me mad."

"All right, we been dogging you," the first rider admitted.

"Why?"

"Because you are on Crown Ranch land."

"From what I hear, I could ride for two or three days and still be on Crown Ranch land," Slocum said.

"That's about the size of it," the first rider said.

Slocum looked at the two men. One of them had a black eye and a badly swollen nose. The other had a bruise on his jaw and a cut and puffed-up lip.

"What the hell happened to you two?" Slocum asked. "Both of you look like you got into a fight with the back end of a mule."

Involuntarily, it seemed, both men touched their wounds.

"He wasn't all that tough," one of them said.

"Who wasn't?"

"Marty," Buck warned. "Shut the hell up."

"Nobody," Marty said, quickly. "What are you doing here, anyway?"

"I'm paying Crown Ranch a friendly visit."

Marty shook his head. "Huh-uh," he said. "We ain't friendly and we don't like visitors."

"That's not very neighborly of you."

"Mister, you'd be a hell of a lot better off if you'd just turn around and go back where you come from," Buck said.

Slocum shook his head. "That's not how it works," he said. He raised his rifle a bit for emphasis. "You see, I'm the one holding the gun here. That means I'm the one giving the orders." He motioned toward the draw with the barrel of his rifle. "Now, my packhorses will be coming out of there directly. How about you fellas picking them up and leading them on into the main house?"

"What are you packing on those animals?"

"Something that belongs to Crown Ranch," Slocum answered.

The first of the four horses appeared then, and Buck looked over toward them.

"Damn, that's Pete," Buck said. "I recognize his boots."

"And that's Sam. What the hell? Who killed these boys?"

"I did," Slocum said.

"You? You're telling me you killed all four of them?"

"All four of them."

"There's no way you could've got all four of 'em without shootin' them in the back."

"If you check, you'll see all the holes are in front," Slocum said.

"You killed them and you're bringin' them in?"

"That's right."

"All I can say about you, mister, is you must be tired of livin'," Buck said.

"You lead the way in," Slocum ordered.

Grumbling, the two cowboys took two horses each and started riding.

It took another hour of steady riding before they reached their destination. The big house was a two-story frame house, but with dormer windows in the roof that suggested either a third story or a finished attic. The house was white, though the shutters and the shake roof were red. It was bracketed by brick chimneys at each end. The chimneys were narrow at the top, but they flared out as they came down the side of the house so that by the time the bricks touched the ground they were nearly three-quarters across each end. Though there were several flowers and shrubs around the house, there was only one tree, a large cottonwood that stood at the northeast corner. In addition to the main house, there was a smaller foreman's house, a bunkhouse, a cookhouse, a granary, and a barn. The granary and cookhouse were somewhat separated from the other buildings because they were built alongside a swiftly flowing stream. The most dominating feature of the granary was its large waterwheel.

A system of flumes, chutes, and pipes brought water from the stream to a water-storage tank in the middle of a wide plaza, and there, at the spigot, Slocum saw a young, very pretty Mexican woman filling a bucket with water. When she looked up, he saw that it was Juanita Arino. The expression on her face was one of quick fear, and he knew that she didn't want him to recognize her, so he gave no hint that he did.

A couple of geese, several chickens, and a handful of guinea hens honked, squawked, and flapped their wings to get out of the way as the little party rode across the wide plaza. A dog, attracted by the scent, ran alongside the horses, yipping at the canvas bundles that were draped across the saddles.

When they drew even with the water tank, Slocum dismounted. He touched the brim of his hat to Juanita in much the way one would greet a stranger. She filled her bucket and turned off the spigot, acknowledging his anonymous greeting with a grateful smile. Then, tossing one last look over her shoulder, she hurried back to the main house. Slocum took down the dipper, filled it, and began drinking, allowing the water to cascade down his mouth to his shirt. As he was drinking a man came out of the main house. The man spoke to the two cowboys Slocum had herded in, then he went over and pulled the canvas aside to look at one of the bodies. When the canvas opened, the smell hit him hard and Slocum saw him jerk his head back quickly, then put a handkerchief to his nose. He made an impatient motion with the back of his hand, said something Slocum was too far away to hear, and the two riders took the four bodies away. The man started toward the water tank.

Slocum took his canteen down from his saddle and held it under the spigot, watching the man come toward him. He had known from the moment he first saw him that it was Caulder. The fact that the sheriff was out here didn't surprise him.

"You got a lot of nerve bringing them out here," Caulder said, nodding toward the withdrawing horses.

"They had to be somewhere," Slocum said. "Couldn't stay in town any longer without getting buried."

"The town has a potter's field," Caulder said.

"Yeah, I know. But since everyone, including you, has gone to such length to tell me that these are Draper's men, I figured the least he would want to do for them is bury them."

"You figured right, Mr. Slocum." This came from a man who was now standing on the front porch of the house. "I'm Seth Draper. Won't you come in?"

"Mr. Draper, I'd better get on back into town," Caulder said.

"Yes, I expect so," Draper said. "Thanks for coming out when I needed you."

"No problem, it's my job," Caulder said.

"I thought he was a town peace officer, not a county sheriff," Slocum said when he stepped inside.

"True, he has no real jurisdiction out here," Draper said. "But without him, I'm afraid we would be without protection. I'm sure you have heard that Caulder works for me?"

"I have heard that."

"I suppose he does, in a way. I pay him to act as a, let us say, private bodyguard. That is in addition to his sheriff's salary. I make no demands of him as far as how he performs his duty for the town of Prosperity; what he does for me is above and beyond that. It is all perfectly legal."

Once inside the house, Slocum looked around. At the back of the room was a stairway, leading up to the second floor. From where he was standing, he could see as far up the stairs as the first landing, but from there the stairs made a sharp turn to the right and he could see no more of it. He turned his attention to the room itself. A large painting hung by wires over a cold fireplace. The painting was of a rather noble-looking figure wearing a colonel's uniform and sitting astride a white horse. The military officer depicted in the picture was Seth Draper.

Seeing him looking at the picture, Draper chuckled. "Oh yes, I'll admit that there is a bit of grandiose pretentiousness in that picture. I mean, to portray myself in uniform suggests that I may have led troops in battle, when the truth of the matter is I have never even been in battle. I'm a colonel in name only, appointed by the military governor of the territory. It is strictly honorary."

"Nice-looking horse," Slocum said, purposely avoiding any comment on Draper's explanation of rank.

"Yes, it is," Draper replied. "Caulder told me what happened to Pete and the others. I can't imagine what got into them. It just doesn't seem like them to try and rob a train like that."

"They weren't trying to rob the train."

"They weren't? But isn't that what you told Caulder last night?"

"I told Caulder they stopped a train, not that they were trying to rob it. Though one of them did decide to help himself from the passengers. What they actually had in mind was to take Mrs. MacTavish," Slocum said. "What were they going to do with her, Draper? Were they going to bring her here?"

Draper went over to a highly polished table and opened a silver case from which he extracted a long, thin cheroot. He struck a match, held it to the end of the cheroot, and puffed until his head was wreathed in tobacco smoke. He studied Slocum through narrowed eyes for a long moment before he spoke.

"Yes," he finally said. "I did want to bring her here. You see, Mr. Slocum, I've been trying to get through to Ian MacTavish that we share a lot of common interests and problems, problems we could solve by cooperation. I'm talking about things like water and grazing rights, land disposition, and our standing together against homesteaders, poachers, and most of all rustlers. I mean it's only right that he and I, as the two biggest landowners in the territory, come to some accord. But Mr. MacTavish doesn't see it as I do. So, I thought perhaps I could convince Mrs. MacTavish to see my side of it; then, hopefully, she could convince Mr. MacTavish."

"So you sent your men to jerk her off the train and bring her to you as your prisoner," Slocum said. "Is that it?"

"Yes. I didn't intend to hurt her, you understand. In fact, I didn't want anyone to get hurt, and I thought this was the only way. I see now what a huge mistake it was, and that mistake cost me the lives of four of my best men. I had no idea she had hired you to ride on that train with her."

"I wasn't working for her," Slocum said. "What I told Caulder was the truth. Your men started shooting at me and I had no choice. I had to shoot back."

"Yes, so I understand. But let me tell you why I am having trouble with that. They were good men, you see," Draper said. "All four of them were crack shots, and it's hard to believe that they could have the drop on you, four to one, and yet when the shooting started, you would come out on top."

"That shouldn't be so hard to believe. I've seen better men and longer odds," Slocum said easily. "And I expect Caulder has, too."

"Yes, I'm quite pleased with Caulder's work. And I think he is pleased with the arrangement he has with me, as well. You could have that same arrangement you know, Mr. Slocum."

"What do you mean?"

"I mean, you could work for me."

"I've got a job," Slocum said.

"Oh? And what would that be?"

"I'm working for Emma MacTavish."

"I thought you said you weren't working for her."

"I wasn't working for her last night. But I am now. It seems that a group of masked riders took her husband from their ranch last night."

"Did they?"

"You don't sound particularly surprised."

"Ian MacTavish is a large rancher. And, like me, he has made more than his share of enemies since he began operating here," Draper said. "I'll be honest with you, there are those who rather resent his European manner-isms. One of his riders left him, to come work for me, as a matter of fact. It isn't all that surprising that someone might wish him harm."

"You wouldn't have any ideas about where he might be, would you?" Slocum asked.

"I'm afraid not."

"I was just thinking, by your own admission you were going to bring Mrs. MacTavish here. Since you failed in that, it doesn't seem that big a stretch to think you might go after Ian MacTavish."

"I don't know what happened to him. But, just to show you that my intentions are in the right place, as far as I'm concerned, if you come to work for me you can continue looking for him, and keep the money she gave you. In fact, I will make finding him your sole responsibility, and I'll double the amount."

"Why would you want to do that?" Slocum asked. "If

I am going to look for him anyway, why would you pay me more to do what I am already doing?"

"Let's just say it is a type of bonus," Draper said. "I would very much like to have you working for me. That way, we could be friends instead of adversaries. I've always thought the best way to control potential enemies is to . . ."

"Buy them?"

"Well, that's a little harsh, really," Draper said. "I was going to say convert them to friends. But, I've found also that spreading a little money around goes a long way toward cementing a friendship."

"It takes more than money to cement a friendship."

Though the cheroot was only smoked halfway down, Draper walked over to an ashtray that was as silver as the case the cheroot had come from and ground it out.

"I know how upset she must be. Please tell her that I am willing to turn loose the biggest army of men this side of Fort Riley, Kansas, to look for him. All she has to do is say the word."

"And turn over the deed to the spring head?" Slocum asked.

"That would seem a fair bargain to me," Draper agreed.

"I'll take your message to her," Slocum said.

After Slocum left, Draper went upstairs to the second floor. Then, reaching up to grab hold of a cord, he pulled down a trapdoor in the ceiling. A ladder slid down and he climbed up the ladder into the attic. The attic was actually one large room, used primarily for storage and illuminated by the light that came in through the dormer windows. In one corner of the attic, and chained to the bed just as Draper had left him, was Ian MacTavish. MacTavish was not only chained to the bed, he was also effectively gagged by means of a sock stuck in his throat, and a cloth tied around his mouth, keeping the sock in place.

Draper walked over to the bed and removed the gag. "Sorry about having to gag you like that, Ian, but I couldn't take a chance on you shouting out while Mr. Slocum was here, could I?"

Ian spit several times in reaction to the sock. Finally he was able to speak. "Who is Slocum?" he asked.

"It's a gunfighter your wife has hired to find you."

Ian smiled. "Good woman," he said. "I didn't think she'd just sit around on her duff waiting for something to happen."

"She may as well have," Draper said. "She is wasting her money with this one. This man she has hired, John Slocum, is nothing but a saddle bum. A saddle bum and a killer. In fact, he killed four of my men last night."

"Did he now? Well then it is nae all a waste, is it?" Ian asked. "A gunfighter, is he?"

"So they say. Much of the town is now wanting to see him and our sheriff fight. I must say, I'm rather looking forward to it myself. I only hope your wife's gunfighter can give Caulder enough of a fight to make it interesting."

10

"Did you see any sign of Ian?" Emma asked.

"No."

"He's there, he has to be. Draper wants that spring head and he doesn't care how he gets it."

"Just because I didn't see him doesn't mean he isn't there," Slocum said. "But Crown Ranch is a big place so there's no telling where he has him. Even if he is in the main house, I am still going to have to find out where he is."

"What is your next move?"

"I think I'll pay Mr. Draper another visit," Slocum said. "Only this time I won't announce it."

"When are you going?"

"When the time is right."

That evening Slocum was sitting at a table in the corner of Manuel's Restaurant having his supper, when a young woman approached his table, carrying a pot of coffee.

"Thanks," Slocum said, pushing his cup toward her.

At that moment the girl looked up, and Slocum saw that it was Juanita.

"Señorita," Slocum said, smiling. "What are you doing here? Have you come to work for Manuel?"

"*Sí,* señor," Juanita said. "Manuel, he is my cousin. He has given me a job because I can work for Señor Draper no more. He is a very evil man."

"Oh? That's not what you said the other day."

"I did not know then what I know now. He has done an evil thing."

"What sort of evil thing?" Slocum was certain that he knew the answer to the question, but he wanted to hear it from another source.

"He has taken Señor MacTavish and is holding him prisoner."

"You've seen MacTavish?"

"*Sí.*"

"Where is he keeping him?"

"He is, how do you say . . . *arriba en el ático*?" Juanita asked.

"The attic?" Slocum asked. "He is upstairs in the attic?"

"*Sí.* He is upstairs in the attic." Tears began to flow from her eyes. "I know Señor MacTavish is a good man because I remember when my cousin, Manuel, work for him. I do not think it is right, what Señor Draper has done."

"How is MacTavish? Is he all right?"

"*Sí,* I think he is not hurt." She smiled through her tears. "But he hurt some of Señor Draper's men, I think. He is a very strong man. He is old, but he is still very *muy macho.*"

Slocum chuckled. "Yeah, I think I saw a couple of the men he may have run into. Buck and Marty."

"*Sí,* Señor Buck, Señor Marty, and Señor Bodine," Juanita said. "You do not think it is wrong of me to come to you?"

"No, I don't think it is wrong at all. You've done the right thing by coming to me," Slocum said. He put his hand on her hand. "And don't worry, señorita. I will get him back."

"*Gracias,* señor."

Juanita turned and started to walk away, but Slocum called out to her.

"*Que?*" she replied, turning back toward him.

Smiling, Slocum held up his coffee cup. "My coffee?" he said.

With an embarrassed laugh, Juanita returned to his table, where she filled his cup.

Half an hour later, Slocum was having a drink at the Red Bull Saloon when the bat-wing doors swung open. Sheriff Caulder, Buck, and Marty came in. The three looked around the room for a moment, then, seeing Slocum at the back, walked to his table. Slocum dropped his right hand to his lap.

"Hello, boys," Slocum said. "Buck, you and Marty really ought to get your faces looked at. I don't know who beat you up but I swear they look worse now than they did this morning. That old man must pack quite a punch."

"He hit me when I wasn't looking," Marty said.

"Marty, shut up," Caulder ordered.

"What brings you three men into Prosperity?" Slocum asked.

"I'm the sheriff here, remember?" Caulder said.

"Oh, I remember, all right," Slocum said. "The question is, do you remember?"

"You just give me some reason to take you to jail and you'll see that I remember," Caulder said.

"I don't plan to give you that reason," Slocum said. "I'm going to be as law-abiding a citizen as anyone you have in this town."

"Mr. Draper says you turned down his offer to work for him," Caulder said. "Is that right?"

"Do you think Draper would lie to you?"

Caulder ignored Slocum's sarcastic remark. "For some reason, Mr. Draper was a little disappointed that you didn't take him up on his offer. But I sure as hell ain't. To me, you're nothing but a saddle bum and a gunny. I used to make my living hunting down people like you."

"Yes, I know," Slocum said. "And you weren't always too particular who you killed, either."

"What the hell is that supposed to mean?"

"I remember a time up in Cheyenne a few years ago, when you brought in a couple of bodies. They were innocent and practically all the paper on them had been pulled, but that didn't stop you."

Caulder stroked his jaw. "Yeah," he said. "I remember that. I chased them for a month and didn't make a dime. How come you know about that?"

"I identified the bodies," Slocum said. "They were friends of mine."

"Is that a fact? Well, you probably don't care all that much for me, do you?"

"I wouldn't say you're high on my list," Slocum replied.

"Then that makes it easy for me to tell you what I got to tell you. Mr. Draper says you ain't welcome out to Crown Ranch anymore."

"Hell, Caulder, what's new about that?" He pointed to Buck and the other rider. "According to these two dumb shits I wasn't welcome the last time."

"Who you callin' a dumb shit?" Buck asked.

"You," Slocum said easily.

"Listen, mister, maybe you ought to know that if I'd known Mr. Draper didn't care whether you was dead or alive, you would've never got the drop on me," Buck growled. "You'd be dead now."

"Enough of that, Buck," Caulder said. He turned back to John. "Slocum, you do understand my message, don't you? If you go out to Crown Ranch again, I'm going to stop you."

"Ian MacTavish is out there, isn't he?"

"What did Draper tell you?"

"He said he wasn't. But I know that he is."

"Well, it really doesn't matter to you, does it?"

"Yeah, it does. I've been paid to bring him back, and I intend to do that."

"From what I understand, if Mrs. MacTavish wants her husband back, all she has to do is pay the price," Caulder said.

"She's already paid the price."

"What do you mean?"

"She paid it to me," Slocum explained. "I'm going to get him back for her."

"Don't try it, Slocum. If you do, we're going to have to fight. And there are too many people in this town who would like to see that. I don't want to kill you, just to provide entertainment for others."

"You don't need to worry none about killin' this fella, Caulder," Buck said. "I'm going to kill him for you."

Caulder looked over at Buck. "You're going to do it?" he scoffed.

"Yeah, I'm going to do it," Buck answered. "He don't look so tough to me. How about it, Mr. Slocum, what do you say? Me and you. You want to try it now? Go for your gun." Buck moved his hand down to hover just over his own gun.

The conversation had started easily enough, but it quickly progressed to a dangerous level, and now a challenge had been issued. From a nearby table a woman's laughter halted in mid-trill and the piano player pulled his hands away from the keyboard so that the last three notes of his melody hung raggedly, discordantly, in the air. All conversation ceased and everyone in the crowded saloon turned to see if the event they had all been speculating on was about to take place. Some of them were disappointed to see that the confrontation was between Slocum and Buck, and not Slocum and Caulder.

"Now, wait a minute, Buck. That is your name, isn't it? Buck?"

"That's the name," Buck said.

"Well, Buck, it wouldn't be a fair draw now, would it?" Slocum asked, replying to the man's challenge. "I mean I'm sitting down, and you're standing up. I would be at a disadvantage trying to draw."

Buck's smile broadened. "Yeah, well, that's the way of it. Sometimes chickens, sometimes feathers. You just got to take it the way it comes. Now, Mr. Slocum. Let's do it now. I told you to go for your gun and I ain't goin' to wait around all night waitin' for you to take me up on it."

Slocum made no move toward his own gun, but he did smile up at Buck and his smile was even colder and more frightening than that of the man who was challenging him.

"Well, Buck, that's the thing of it. I don't have to go for my gun. I already have it out. You see, I figured you might try some dumb-fool stunt like this, so I got ready for you. I'm holding a gun under this table right now and it's pointed straight at your gut."

Buck blinked a couple of times, then he laughed nervously. "Who the hell are you trying to kid, mister?" he asked. "You ain't got no gun in your hand." With his left hand, he pointed. "Hell, I can see your gun in your holster, plain as day!"

"Really? Well, I'm not talking about that gun," Slocum explained. "What I'm talking about is the holdout gun I keep up my sleeve. It's a Derringer, two barrels, forty-one caliber. I can shoot right through this table and put a hole in your belly big enough to reach in and pull your guts out. Well, you know what one just like it did to Abraham Lincoln."

"You're bluffin'. You ain't got no holdout gun under there. I know you ain't."

"You may be right," Slocum admitted. "Could be that there's nothing under here. Or, could be that it's just what I said it was."

"You expect me to believe you?"

"No, Buck. I expect you to die. Go ahead, try it now and let's get this over with so I can shoot you, then get back to my drinking."

Buck stood his ground for a moment longer, trying to decide whether or not he would call Slocum's bluff. His eyes narrowed, a muscle in his cheek twitched, and sweat broke out on his forehead.

"What are you going to do now, Buck?" Marty asked.

"I don't know," Buck admitted. "I don't know. Caulder, what do you think? You've been in these kinds of situations before. Does this son of a bitch have a holdout gun under the table or doesn't he?"

"I doubt it," Caulder said.

"Ha!" Buck smiled. "I didn't think so. Come on, Caulder, let's me and you call his bluff."

"Uh-uh," Caulder replied, shaking his head. "You started it. You call his bluff."

"But you said he doesn't have a gun under there."

"No. What I said was, I doubt it. I don't know whether he has one or not. I do know I'm not going to call his bluff."

"You mean you're just going to hang me out to dry, here?" Buck asked, nervously.

"It's not my fight," Caulder replied.

"Marty? How about you? You going to help me here?"

"Leave me out of it," Marty said. "This is all your doin'."

"Shit!" Buck shouted. He put his hands out in front of him. "All right, all right, I ain't goin' to go for my gun now," he said. He pointed at Slocum. "But you and me has got us a score to settle, mister. And I don't plan on just waitin' around till you come onto Crown Ranch before it's settled."

"Come on, Buck, Marty, let's get out of here," Caulder ordered.

"Caulder?" Slocum called out as the three men started to leave. Caulder turned toward Slocum.

"You tell Draper that I know he has MacTavish out there. And I know where he is keeping him. I'll give him until seven o'clock tomorrow morning to get him back to his wife. If he hasn't done it by then, I'm coming out there again. Only this time, it won't be a friendly visit."

"I don't think you want to do that, Slocum," Caulder replied ominously.

"I'm going to do it."

"You're just one man. What do you expect to do?"

"I expect to make Draper's life so miserable that when I finally send that sorry son of a bitch to hell, he'll welcome the change."

"Do you think that's supposed to scare Mr. Draper?" Buck growled.

Caulder waved Buck quiet. "Shut up, Buck," he said. He turned to Slocum. "Don't be a fool, Slocum. Don't you know that if you come out there, I'm going to have to kill you?"

"I know you are going to try," Slocum replied. "But you have to know, also, that I'm going to try, just as hard, not to get killed."

"You'll lose, Slocum. We'll have an army waiting for you."

"If your army is no better than these two, you sure won't have much."

"You son of a bitch!" Buck started, but Caulder reached out to grab him.

"That's enough," Caulder said. "We've got to get back to the ranch. We've got to make preparations for our . . ."

He paused and smiled without mirth at Slocum. ". . . visitor," he concluded, letting the word slide out slowly.

Slocum watched until all three men had disappeared through the swinging bat-wing doors. Then he brought his hands up from under the table. They were completely empty. When the others in the saloon saw this, they burst out into loud, raucous laughter. Some applauded.

Smiling to acknowledge their applause, Slocum got up from the table and walked over to the bar. He handed the bartender his empty mug, requesting a refill, and as Jeb walked down to the beer barrel to refill the mug, Slocum leaned over the bar, reached underneath, and took out the Greener double-barrel, ten-gauge, sawed-off shotgun. Cocking it, he pointed it at the door. Then, calmly, he waited.

"You son of a bitch!" Buck shouted, suddenly darting back inside the door. His gun was in his hand and he fired a shot at the table where Slocum had been a moment earlier. His bullet crashed into the mug of beer the piano player had sitting on top of his upright, sending up a shower of glass and amber fluid. The piano player, suddenly finding himself in the middle of a gunfight, dived to the floor and scooted underneath the nearest table.

"I'm over here, Buck," Slocum said calmly, standing at the bar.

Then, realizing that Slocum had moved, Buck located him at the bar and swung his pistol around for a second shot.

He didn't get a second shot off.

Slocum pulled both triggers on the shotgun and it boomed loudly, filling the saloon with smoke. The double-aught buckshot turned Buck's head and upper torso into ground sausage, and he was slammed back against the bat-wing doors with such force as to tear them off the hinges. He landed on his back at the far side of the boardwalk with what was left of his head halfway down the steps.

Slocum lay the still-smoking shotgun down on the bar, then walked to the front of the saloon where he stood in the wrecked doorway, looking down at Buck's body. Though he no longer had the shotgun, he did have his pistol in his hand, a fact that didn't go unnoticed by Sheriff Caulder.

There were heavy footfalls on the boardwalk as Deputy Boyle came running up to the saloon. Seeing Slocum standing over Buck's body, he stopped.

"I don't reckon I even need to ask who done this," he said.

"I did it," Slocum replied easily.

"I hate to admit it, Percy, but Slocum didn't have no choice," Caulder said. "I couldn't hold Buck back. He was bound and determined to gun him down."

"So, you don't want me to arrest him?" Percy asked. The relief in his voice was so obvious that some, among the crowd who had gathered, giggled.

"No need," Caulder said. He stroked his chin and sighed. "All right," he said. "Couple of you men get this stiff down to the undertaker's establishment." He looked over at Slocum. "You and me are going to have to get this settled pretty soon," he said. "You're hard on the population."

11

When Julie came into Slocum's room that night, he was expecting her. He hadn't totally thrown caution to the winds, after all he had made a few enemies since arriving, so he did have his pistol cocked and aimed at the door as she opened it and slipped inside. When he saw that it was her, he lowered the hammer, then put the gun down. She never realized she had been a target.

"John?" she called quietly. "John, are you awake?"

"I'm here," Slocum said. He turned up the lantern, filling the room with light.

Julie moved across the floor quickly, then set on the edge of the bed. "I heard about what happened in the saloon tonight," she said.

"I figured you would have. When things like that happen, word gets around."

"I worry about you."

"Don't."

"No, I'm serious. I do worry about you," Julie said.

"And I'm serious when I say don't," Slocum said. "A man who lives the way I do can't afford to have someone worrying about him. Especially a woman."

"Why, that's the silliest thing I've ever heard."

"No, it isn't at all silly," Slocum said. "You have to understand, Julie, I live my entire life in the moment. There are no memories, and there is no future. There is only now. That gives me an edge . . . the edge I need to stay alive. And if I ever started worrying about what my getting killed would mean for anyone else, I would lose that edge."

"Oh," Julie said, in a plaintive voice.

"You do understand, don't you?"

"I . . . I guess so," she said. "But, what an awful way that is to live."

"No," Slocum said. "It's not at all an awful way. You have to understand, Julie, that if your entire life is in the moment, then everything you experience, everything you feel, is larger than life. Like, what I feel for you, right now."

"Oh?" Her tone brightened. "And what do you feel for me, right now?"

"You are making this moment complete for me."

Julie turned the sheet down, then looked up with a quizzical smile on her face. "You're naked," she said. "Do you always sleep naked?"

"Not always." He smiled. "But I figured you would be paying me a visit tonight."

"Pretty sure of yourself, aren't you?"

"Let's just say I was very hopeful, and I wanted to be prepared."

Julie let her hand trail down his stomach, across the wiry bush of hair, then to his cock, which was standing straight up. Slowly, tentatively, she wrapped her fingers around it. "Oh, you are prepared," she said.

"That part was easy," Slocum replied.

Standing up, Julie slipped out of her nightgown, then, also naked, sat back on the bed. "I'm the one who talked Aunt Emma into staying in town until we get Uncle Ian back," she said. "I did that because I wanted to see you again. Is that wicked of me?"

"Wicked? No, I would just say that is clever. It did allow us this time together again."

Slocum reached up to touch her, letting his fingers pass across silky smooth skin, tracing a path from her shoulder to the curve of a breast, then out to a hard, little nipple. He rubbed it gently.

"John, I think you ought to know. You're . . . you're not the first man I have been with," she said.

"It doesn't matter. You are with me now."

"I don't know why, I felt I had to tell you. I know nothing will ever come of this. It's just that, well, I can't deceive you."

Slocum put his arms around Julie and drew her close to him. Her lips came to his and he parted them with his tongue. She didn't retreat from him, but met his tongue with her own in a tangling duet of taste and texture. She was a woman, by her own admission, of experience, and, by Slocum's own knowledge, of passion, and she responded to him like a wild animal, writhing, moaning, and flailing her hands about his body. Slocum moved his mouth from her lips and began kissing her on the neck, sucking the flesh up into his mouth and biting it.

Julie increased the tempo of her movements, running her hands up and down his back as if she were looking for a handhold. Slocum pinched the lobe of her ear gently between his lips, then stuck his tongue in her ear. He saw her nipple in the soft, silver glow of the moonlight, straining as if it were trying to open. He put her breast in his mouth, then rubbed her other nipple with the tips of his fingers.

"Oh," Julie said, almost whimpering with the joy of it. "Oh, it's wonderful . . . it's so wonderful."

Slocum moved from breast to breast with his mouth, then sought out the other parts of her body. His head slid

down across her stomach, then he kissed her on the inside
of each thigh. He felt her legs tremble uncontrollably. Her
moans of pleasure turned into cries for release.

"Oh, John, now, please, now! Don't make me wait any
longer!"

Slocum felt as if his very blood had turned to boiling
oil. Every inch of his body was sensitized to pleasure. He
moved up and spread her legs, then came down on her,
pushing his throbbing cock into the hot, wet cavern of her
cunt. He began pushing it in and pulling it out, mining
the deepest part of her. Then, he felt her climax around
him, barking her pleasure as with big sporadic jerks she
gave herself over to the release she had attained.

Slocum couldn't hold back any longer, and he felt himself escaping through that part of him that was joined with
Julie. For a fleeting instant, he tried to hold back, then he
gave up, and with a final thrust, purged his body of the
escaping energy. He could feel the extreme sensitivity of
Julie's breasts, and the completeness of the pleasure she
had just attained.

After a few moments, Julie's hand began roaming
again. They found Slocum, now in a flaccid state, and
with a few expert strokes, soon had him erect again. This
time, they weren't quite as hungry and Slocum was able
to coast up to the edge of a climax, revel in the delightful
sensations, then back away from it without going over the
edge. They kept this up for a long time: slow, pleasurable
strokes, exchanged kisses, and the sensitized contact of
naked skin against naked skin.

Manuel had offered Juanita a bed in his house but had
she accepted, she would have put the children out. She
made arrangements with the hotel to rent her room not by
the night but by the month, thus making the rates reasonable enough for her to afford. What she did not realize,

when she took the room, was that it was right across the hall from Slocum's room.

She didn't know how long she had been asleep when something awakened her. It may have been a noise, though as she lay in bed listening, she heard nothing. She had almost decided it was nothing but a dream and had closed her eyes to go back to sleep when she heard a distinct sound. It was a woman's voice, and the woman had cried out. But there was something strange about the cry. It wasn't a cry of fear or pain. It was a cry unlike anything Juanita had ever heard before, and yet, though it was new to her, she realized instinctively that it was a cry of passion and pleasure.

The sound had a disquieting effect on Juanita, and she turned over, hoping to find a position that would blot out the sound. When she did turn over she made an amazing discovery. Juanita gasped as she saw, reflected in the propped-open transom glass above her door, the very thing that had caused the cry of passion. By some optical trick Juanita's transom was picking up the reflection of the transom across the hallway. As clearly as if she were looking in a mirror, Juanita could see into the room across the hallway, where the lamp was burning brightly and a scene of passion was being played out by Slocum and Julie MacTavish. Juanita was, by chance, thrust into the role of unwitting witness to their lovemaking.

Juanita could see as clearly as if she were actually in the room with them. She could hear as well, for neither Slocum nor Julie made any effort to be quiet. The bed-coverings had been cast aside, and two naked figures were clearly visible on the bed. Julie lay with her legs wantonly spread, and Juanita could see a dark tangle of hair and a pink, glistening cleft. But it was not the woman who held her attention. It was the man, for Juanita was seeing John Slocum fully aroused, and it made quite an imposing sight.

The two naked bodies came together on the bed, kissing each other in a strange mixture of tenderness and savage fury. As she watched, her own breath began coming in gasps as short and desperate as the breathing of the man and woman on the bed in the other room.

Juanita was puzzled by the heat she felt. A moment before it had been cool enough to require a sheet, now she cast the sheet aside because she was swept by such heat that she began to perspire. Her sleeping gown had worked its way up her legs, and she felt an unaccustomed breath of air on her bare legs, though the breeze did little to cool the heat that now blazed unchecked in her loins.

Steadily the moans of the man and woman grew louder and more urgent, while their thrashing became more frenzied. Then they seemed to reach an apex of some sort, a pinnacle of savage tenderness that brought louder and more intense little cries and grunts from both of them. Then, strangely, there was a prolonged stillness, and the two lay in each other's arms. Juanita, who was alone in her own bed, felt a devastating sense of emptiness at that moment. She wished she had not been a witness to the scene. Despite that wish, she was much too absorbed to turn away, even now, when it was finished.

She watched until Julie left, and John turned out the lantern, putting the room into darkness so that she could see no more.

Slocum was on his father's farm back in Georgia. He was fishing in the creek, and though he was as old as he is now, everyone else around him was as they were then. He had not yet realized this was a dream, and he was trying to make sense of this strange event when his mother turned to speak to him.

"John!"

The warning cry cut through the layers of sleep as quickly as a knife through hot butter. The dream fell away and Slocum, with reflexes born of years of living on the edge, rolled off the bed just as a gun boomed in the doorway of his room. The bullet slammed into the headboard of the bed where, but a second earlier, Slocum had been sleeping.

At the same time Slocum rolled off the bed, he grabbed the pistol from under his pillow. Now the advantage was his. The man who had attempted to kill him was temporarily blinded by the muzzle flash of his own shot and he could see nothing in the darkness of Slocum's room. That same muzzle flash, however, had illuminated the assailant for Slocum and he quickly aimed his pistol at the dark hulk in the doorway, closed his eyes against his own muzzle flash, and squeezed the trigger. The gun bucked in his hand as the roar filled the room.

To Slocum there was a measurable amount of time between the explosion of the intruder's gun and his own. To others in the hotel, or in the nearby buildings, however, the two shots came so close together as to be almost simultaneous. In the town of Prosperity, drunken patrons of the saloons often vented their spirits with the discharge of pistols. But the citizens of the town had learned to recognize the difference in the sound made by those shots fired in play and shots that were fired in anger. Everyone within hearing knew that these were angry shots. A few of the more pious breathed little prayers as they realized that someone had just died.

Slocum heard a groaning sound, then the heavy thump of a falling body.

"John! John! Are you all right?" Julie asked in a frightened voice. It had been Julie's warning shout that he awakened Slocum in time to avoid being killed in his bed.

"What is it? What's happening?" another voice called. All up and down the hallway of the hotel, doors opened as patrons, dressed in nightgowns and pajamas peered out of their rooms in curiosity. Emma MacTavish came running up the hall to stand beside her granddaughter. The two women stood arm in arm, looking down at the man who, lighted by the hall lamps, lay dead on the floor.

Slipping on his trousers, but naked from the waist up, Slocum stepped out into the hallway, then looked down at the body of the man he had just killed.

"It's Marty," Slocum said. He sighed. "I had a run-in with his partner earlier tonight."

"Damn, mister, the sheriff was right!" one of the patrons said. Dressed in his sleeping gown and nightcap, he had come from his room and was now standing over the body. "You are hard on the population."

"He had no choice," Julie explained. "The man was trying to kill him."

"I appreciate the warning," Slocum said. "How did you happen to see him?"

"I heard someone walking by our door," Julie said. "I don't know, I just had a feeling that whoever it was was up to no good. So I opened the door a crack and looked out. When I did, I saw that he was standing just outside your door, with his gun drawn."

"How did he get in?" the man in the nightcap asked. "Do you keep your door unlocked?"

Slocum looked over at Julie. She had left his room no more than an hour earlier, and, evidently, had not relocked the door. She flushed slightly, under his gaze. Her reaction didn't go unnoticed by Emma MacTavish.

"I reckon I just forgot to lock it," Slocum said.

"Too bad. If your door had been locked, no doubt this wouldn't have happened."

"It would've happened," Slocum said easily. "Maybe not tonight, but it would have happened."

"What are you going to do about him now?" the hotel patron asked.

"Nothing," Slocum said. "I don't need to do anything about him now. He's dead."

"Well, good Lord, man, you don't plan to just leave him out here, do you? I mean, how do you think any of the rest of us are going to be able to sleep, knowing there is a dead man lying out in the hall."

"If you want him out of here, take him out of here," Slocum said.

"The hell you say. I didn't kill him."

"He's got a point there, mister," one of the others said. "You killed him. The least you can do is get rid of him."

"Wait a minute, none of you are being fair," Julie said. "Mr. Slocum didn't invite this man up here."

"Nevertheless, he's here, and he's dead," the man in the nightgown said. "And this man is responsible. I say it is also his responsibility to get rid of him."

"No problem," Slocum said. Leaning down, he picked Marty up and threw his body over his shoulder.

"That's more like it," the man in the nightgown said.

Without another word, Slocum walked to the rear end of the hall. When he passed the stairs the people began mumbling to one another.

"Wait a minute, you went past the stairs," someone said.

"What are you doing with him? Where are you going?" another called.

At the end of the hall, Slocum raised the window that opened out onto the alley.

"Hey! What are you . . . ?"

That was as far as the nightgown man got, because without any further hesitation, Slocum pushed Marty's body through the window. It fell with a crash to the alley below. That done, he lowered the window then, brushing his hands as if having just completed an onerous task, returned to his own room.

"That should take care of it," Slocum said. "Sleep well, everyone."

"That was no way to handle that!" the man in the sleeping gown complained. "I've a good mind to—"

"Go back to bed," Slocum said.

"What?" the man sputtered. "See here, you can't . . ."

"Does this loudmouthed gentleman belong to any of you ladies?" Slocum asked, pointedly. "If so, I strongly recommend that you call him back to bed."

"Herbert, come back to bed," a woman called from a half-opened doorway down the hall.

"I will not be ordered around like some—"

"I said, come back to bed!" the woman said, much more forcefully this time.

Mumbling, Herbert straightened his sleeping cap to recover as much dignity as he could, then walked back down the hallway to his wife.

"I would suggest all of you go back to bed," Slocum said. "The show is over."

As everyone began going back to their rooms, Slocum glanced across the hallway and saw Juanita standing just inside her room with the door half open.

"Juanita!" John said, surprised to see her. "You are staying here in the hotel now?"

"*Si*. I live here now," Juanita said.

"I'm sorry about the spectacle."

"The spectacle?" Juanita gasped. "You knew that I could see?"

"See? See what?" Slocum asked, confused by her strange reaction.

Subconsciously, Juanita looked up at the open transom over the door that led into John's room. Then, quickly, as if she didn't want him to know what she was looking at, she glanced away.

Still confused, John looked up at his transom. Though his bed was illuminated only by the ambient light that spilled in from the hallway, John could see it quite clearly in his transom. Then, looking across the hall at Juanita's transom, he saw his bed reflected there as well. Suddenly he realized the implications and he looked steadily at Juanita, who now realized that Slocum knew. He saw her flush a bright crimson.

"Good night, señor," she said, closing the door quickly before he could say anything else to her.

"I'll be damned," Slocum said to himself.

"It's a good thing you heard someone walking by our door, dear," Emma said, after she and Julie returned to their room and prepared for bed.

"Yes, it is. Slocum could have been killed."

"You should have been more careful when you left his room," Emma said. "You should have made certain the door was locked."

Julie gasped. "You . . . you knew I was down there?"

"Not only tonight, my dear, but last night as well."

"You knew, but you said nothing."

Emma chuckled. "Darling, if I were a bit younger, and unmarried, I might be giving you a little competition with this gentleman."

"Aunt Emma!" Julie gasped.

"Just because I'm old, dear, doesn't mean I don't have an appreciation for a good-looking man. It is just that my opportunities to do anything about it are much more limited these days."

"You . . . you are bad!" Julie said, breaking into laughter.

"Oh, yes," Emma replied. "And in my younger days, when I was bad . . . I was very good."

Others on the floor of the hotel wondered at the incongruity of the laughter coming from one of the rooms after something like this.

12

Slocum was awakened the next morning by the sound of a train whistle. Getting up, he dressed, then moved along the upstairs hallway, passed Emma and Julie's room, then passed all the other doors where he could hear the snores and heavy breathing of the other guests, still asleep in their rooms. As he walked down the stairway the cacophony of snoring gradually fell behind him to be replaced the measured ticktock of the clock in the hotel lobby. Its workings sounded exceptionally loud in the early morning silence. The clock showed that it was ten minutes until six. That meant Slocum had time to eat breakfast before the seven o'clock deadline he had given Draper to return Ian MacTavish.

As Slocum left the saloon he saw the train that had awakened him. The locomotive sat hissing and popping while its smokestack spewed forth a billowing cloud of black smoke. This was a freight train and already several wagons were in line, waiting for their turn. Some were taking cargo from the train, others were putting cargo on.

When Slocum went into the café, he saw that there were only four other customers at this early hour. Two of them were teamsters whose wagon, standing in front of the café, had not yet joined the queue down at the depot. The other two diners were a couple of drummers, waiting for the morning stage. Their sample cases sat on the floor beside them.

Slocum ordered a stack of pancakes, two eggs, a large piece of ham, biscuits, and red-eye gravy. It was a large breakfast, but when he was on the trail he ate so irregularly and modestly that he tended to make up for it when the opportunity presented itself. He was halfway through his breakfast when someone opened the door of the café and called out to the two teamsters.

"Ernie, Phil? All the rest of the wagons are gone. They're ready for you guys if you want to move your wagon down there now."

"All right, we'll be right there," one of them said, finishing his coffee in one big swig.

"What's gon' on, Ernie? You two boys know someone in the railroad to have a special invitation like that?" one of the drummers teased.

"Nothin' special about it," Ernie answered. "We're just pickin' up a load of dynamite, that's all. Nobody else likes to be around when that stuff is being handled."

"Yeah," Phil added, laughing. "We got a free breakfast out of it. The other drivers got together and bought our breakfast if we'd agree to wait until they were gone."

"You say you're handling dynamite? Well, I can't see as I blame them for wantin' to be out of there before you started," the drummer said.

"Oh, dynamite's not bad," Ernie said. "I mean, it ain't like handlin' nitro. You gotta really be careful with that stuff."

John lingered over his breakfast for another twenty minutes or so, drinking two extra cups of coffee. He had sent word to Draper that he would give him until seven o'clock, and he intended to do just that. Of course, he had sent word through Caulder, Buck, and Marty. But he killed Buck and Marty last night, so if Caulder didn't get word to him, then Draper wouldn't know about the deadline. However, that was Draper's problem, not his.

Checking the clock on the wall of the café, John pulled out his own pocket watch to compare the two. They were within a minute of each other, indicating fifteen minutes until seven. He put money on the table to pay for his breakfast, then stood up. He harbored no false hope that Draper would be here with Ian MacTavish, but he intended to be out in the street in plenty of time to meet him, just as if he believed it might actually happen.

Just down the street from the café, in front of the Prosperity Emporium, the two teamsters who had been at breakfast a few minutes earlier had already taken the cargo off the train and were now unloading their wagon. From the delicate way they were handling the boxes, Slocum knew it was the dynamite they had been talking about.

"John!" a woman's voice shouted, and John looked around to see Mrs. MacTavish coming toward him, moving as quickly as she could. "John, come quick!"

For a moment Slocum entertained the thought that maybe Draper had delivered Mr. MacTavish, but the tone in her voice was more of anguish than of joy. He started toward her.

"What is it?" he asked. "What's wrong?"

"It's Dan," Mrs. MacTavish said. "I let him stay in the car last night."

Slocum followed her back to the rail spur. Even before he got there, though, he could see a crowd of people standing around, looking down at something on the ground just under the private car. When he was close enough, he saw that it was a body. Dan's body.

"When did this happen?" Slocum asked.

"I don't know," Mrs. MacTavish said. "I came down

here from the hotel to tell Dan some things I wanted him to do out at the ranch and I saw him here, like this."

Leaning down, Slocum put his hand on Dan's cheek. The skin was cold. When he tried to lift an arm, it was stiff. Rigor mortis was already setting in.

"It could have happened almost anytime during the night," Slocum said. "Lying down here like this, he wouldn't be visible to anyone unless they came right up to him."

"Poor Dan."

Slocum turned Dan over. There was a knife sticking out of his chest and the people who were standing around gasped when they saw it. Their gasps turned to exclamations of surprise and curiosity, however, when they saw that the knife was sticking through a note.

Slocum removed the knife and read the note: *"Mrs. MacTavish, if you want to see your husband alive, you are going to have to pay the price."*

"Oh, my," Emma said. She began dabbing at her eyes. "Oh, my, now we have caused this. Poor Dan. How could I have let something like this happen to him?"

"You didn't do this to him," Slocum said. "Draper did it. Or he had it done, and that's the same thing."

"How could anyone do this?" she asked.

"You would be surprised at how easy this is for some people," Slocum said. He folded the note and put it in his pocket.

"Make way! Make way, here! Let me through!" Deputy Boyle shouted as he pushed his way through the crowd. When he saw Slocum, he let out a long, exasperated sigh. "Goddammit, Slocum, what the hell is it with you? Everywhere you go somebody turns up dead. Buck, last night in the saloon, then Marty, in the middle of the night, and now this. I suppose you did this as well. And I guess, like the others, you were forced into it."

"I didn't do this."

"Then who did?"

"You might ask your boss," Slocum said, showing Percy the note.

"I'm askin' you."

"Oh, for crying out loud, Boyle, you know we didn't have anything to do with this."

"Is Caulder still in town?" Slocum asked.

Percy shook his head. "I ain't seen him since the little fracas in the saloon last night."

"I'm sure I'll see him out at Crown Ranch," Slocum said.

"You're going out there?" Percy asked.

"Yes."

"I wouldn't do that if I was you."

"He's going to run an errand for me," Emma said.

"Uh-huh, some errand. You're going to get yourself killed, that's what you're going to do. And I don't want it said that I didn't warn you."

"You warned me," Slocum said.

Percy stood there for a moment, glaring at Slocum. It was obvious he would like to arrest Slocum, even if he had to trump up the charge. But it was equally as obvious that he was frightened of Slocum, so he would do nothing on his own.

The undertaker arrived then, and looked down at the body.

"Damn, Welch, if this keeps on, you're going to have to start paying a bonus to this fella here on all the bodies that turn up," Deputy Doyle said.

"Business has been good since he arrived," Welch agreed. "Will the city be paying for this?"

"No, I'll pay for it," Emma said. "Dan worked for Cross Pass."

"Then you'll be wanting the best for him, I suppose," Welch said. "I have just received a new model casket, called Eternal Cloud. It's black with silver trim, oh, it's quite lovely, a work of art, really."

"Your regular coffin will do," Emma said. "Dan wasn't a man given to geegaws and such."

"Yes, ma'am," Welch said, obviously disappointed at not making the sale.

"All right, folks," Deputy Boyle said. "You can break it up now. Go on about your business, the show's over."

As the crowd started to leave, Emma called Slocum to one side so she could speak to him privately. "Mr. Slocum, I told you I would pay you fifteen hundred dollars to bring Ian back," she said. "I want him alive and unhurt, but, if for some reason you can't do that then I'll pay the fifteen hundred dollars, plus a thousand dollar bonus to see Seth Draper dead."

"I don't kill for hire, Mrs. MacTavish," Slocum said.

"And I'm not hiring you to kill him," Emma said. "I'm just putting a bounty on him, that's all. I know you are not opposed to accepting a bounty. Had there been one on those four men you killed who attacked the train, you would have collected it. This is just a bounty you can collect if you kill Seth Draper."

"That's a pretty narrow point," Slocum suggested.

"Yes, I agree," Emma replied. She smiled coldly. "But then you might say that I am a narrow-minded woman. I want that man dead."

"I'm sure you do. But don't forget, there's a man standing between Draper and me who might have other ideas."

"You are talking about Caulder."

"I am."

"How loyal do you think he would really be, if it came right down to it?" Emma asked.

"Loyalty has nothing to do with it," Slocum replied. "For Caulder, Draper is the goose that is laying the golden eggs. He isn't going to want to see that goose killed. Also,

I'm pretty sure that he is getting more and more curious as to which of us is the better man."

"You're better than Caulder, aren't you?" Emma asked anxiously.

"I don't know," Slocum admitted. "But I guess we are going to find out."

It took Slocum less than five minutes to saddle his horse and about ten more minutes to pick up a few supplies at the emporium. The storekeeper raised his eyes at some of the items, then raised them again when Slocum told him to send the bill to Emma MacTavish, care of Cross Pass Station, but he kept his curiosity to himself. What did he care what Slocum did with his strange purchases, so long as he got paid? And there was no more solid account in the area than the Cross Pass Station account.

When Slocum rode out of town a few minutes later, he had everything he needed to wage war against Crown Ranch.

13

"I want a lookout posted in the loft of the barn at all times," James Caulder said. "And I want another one on top of the big house. Also, get somebody to build a little shelf up in the cottonwood tree by the corner of the building where that attic room is."

Caulder was standing on the plaza at Crown Ranch, looking up at a rider named Barney. Barney was Buck's brother and aching for revenge against Slocum. That made him a motivated warrior for Caulder.

"Hell, what do we need all that for, Caulder? We already got somebody down at the pass," Barney replied. He reached down and patted his horse's neck. "There ain't nobody that can get through there without us knowing about it. I say let's just wait down there and blast him when he tries to come through."

"Do it," Caulder said without elaboration. "And the barn, too. I want one man in the loft and another on the roof. Now, what about the rifle pits? How are they coming?"

Barney laughed. "What's all the fuss, Caulder? You act like we was about to get attacked by an army or somethin'. Lookouts, rifle pits. You sure you don't have a couple of cannons hid out some'ers?"

"Believe me, if I had them, I would use them," Caulder replied. "And as far as you're concerned, Slocum is an army. A one-man army."

"Shit, he ain't no different from anyone else. I'll bet you're faster'n he is. And anyway, when it comes right down to it, he puts his pants on one leg at a time just like ever'one else."

"How do you know that?" Caulder replied. "You ever see him put his pants on?"

"What? Well, no, but . . ."

"Then don't assume a goddamn thing, including don't assume that I'm faster'n he is."

"Are you afraid of him, Caulder?" Barney asked in surprise.

"You goddamn right I'm afraid of him. You would be, too, if you had any sense. Your brother wasn't afraid of him, and look where it got him and Marty. I warned those two crazy bastards but they wouldn't listen to me and now they're dead."

"But, you're the Widow Maker. You're faster than he is," Barney insisted. "I mean, ever'body says that."

"Do they?"

"Well, aren't you?"

"I'm going to let you in on a little secret," Caulder said. "Most people have to think about it before they kill someone. I don't. And while they are thinking about it, I'm doing it. That's the advantage a professional gunfighter has over the average person. Slocum isn't the average person. He doesn't have to think about it, either. That takes away the edge, and I don't like going into a fight where I don't have the edge. Now, get busy."

"All right, all right," Barney said. "I'll get the lookouts all posted like you told me, and I'll see to it that the rifle pits are dug. And, if you want me to, I'll see if I can find a cannon or two for you."

"Just do it," Caulder growled.

Caulder watched Barney ride off, then he heard someone walking up behind him. As quick as a flash of lightning, he drew his pistol and whirled around with his gun in his hand.

"Whoa!" Draper said, holding out his hands. "You are really spooked."

"Don't ever walk up behind me like that again," Caulder warned.

"You keep on talking to people the way you were talking to Barney, and you are going to scare everyone to death," Draper said. He lit a cheroot, then shook the match out before he tossed it away.

"I want everyone to be afraid of him," Caulder said. "I want them to think he's part grizzly bear, part mountain lion, and part Apache, all rolled into one."

"Is he really all that good?"

"Don't forget, I've seen him work. He's good. He's damn good."

"But, he hasn't really stood up to anyone, has he?" Draper asked. "I mean, those men on the train, it wasn't a matter of who drew first. Same with the business in the saloon last night. From what you told me, Slocum was standing over at the bar when Buck came in, blazing away. Slocum killed him with a shotgun. Then, last night, in the hotel, that was a shoot-out in the dark, so it wasn't a matter of who was fastest, either, was it?"

"What's your point?" Caulder asked.

"Well, my point is, you are good with a gun," Draper said. "You are good, and you are fast. Very fast. In my book, there is no comparing the two of you. Besides which, I've never even heard of John Slocum."

"When somebody is as good as Slocum is and you don't know it, that gives him a big edge. And the fact

that he can keep himself off the reward dodgers and out
of newspapers . . . that just shows how smart he is."

"It's too bad," Draper said.

"What's too bad?"

"It's too bad we couldn't talk him into working for us.
Especially if he's as good as you say he is. If he is the
best."

Caulder pulled the makings out of his pocket and began
rolling a cigarette.

"I didn't say he was the best," Caulder said as he sprin-
kled tobacco into the paper. "He's damn good," he added
as he licked the paper and rolled it closed, twisting each
end. "But the question of who is the best . . ." He struck
a match with his thumbnail and began puffing until the
cigarette was lit, then he blew out a long cloud of aromatic
smoke before he continued. ". . . is still unanswered."

"Well, then, who do you think is the best?" Draper
asked.

"Whoever is left alive when this is over," Caulder said.

Early the next morning, like every morning, the cook at
Crown Ranch made biscuits for breakfast, rolled dough
for bread for the rest of the day, peeled potatoes, carved
meat, cleaned the stove, and attended to the dozen or more
other duties for which he was responsible. By the time
the other hands were sitting down for their breakfast, the
cook was already three hours into his day.

On this morning the cook put the bacon, eggs, potatoes,
biscuits, and coffee on the table so the men could help
themselves. With that taken care of, he took a couple of
sheets of old newspaper with him and started out to the
toilet. The newspaper would give him something to read
while he was attending to his business, and, of course,
would come in handy afterward.

The outhouse was on the other side of the stream, away
from the water so as not to contaminate it. Unlike most

of the other ranches in the area, Crown Ranch enjoyed an ample supply of water. That was because of the dozen or more streams and tributaries that branched off from the Wahite River. These streams and tributaries weren't natural offshoots from the river: they had been created when Draper dammed up the river. Normally, such a dam would have backed the water up until a large lake was formed, but that was prevented by a system of sluices and gates that rerouted the water.

This elaborate water system was good for Crown Ranch, for it brought water to even the most remote part of the ranch. However, it was bad for the other ranchers and farmers in the valley because the same dam that created the Crown Ranch irrigation system caused the Wahite to stop flowing. No one downstream of Crown Ranch, not one rancher, received so much as one drop of water from the Wahite. In fact, Draper had built both the cookhouse and granary right in the dry riverbed through which the Wahite once flowed. A small tributary still managed to get through, and by building the granary there, Draper could harness its energy to turn the waterwheel that ground his grain. The little stream also provided the water the cook needed to run his kitchen, and fed the water tank in the middle of the plaza. It was that same stream the cook crossed when he left the kitchen to go to the toilet.

The cook had been sitting in the toilet for a few minutes when he heard the sound. It sounded a little like thunder, deep and resonant, way up in the hills. And yet it wasn't quite like thunder; it had a flatter, more immediate sound. Besides, there wasn't a cloud in the sky.

There was another thump soon after the first, and this time it made the hairs stand up on the back of the cook's neck. That was because he had heard a sound like this during the war. This sounded exactly like artillery! But that was crazy! Why would anyone be shooting out here?

The cook made a quick, final use of the paper, then

stepped out of the toilet and looked up toward the hills. He saw an ominous little puff of smoke hanging just on the other side of one of the notches in the hills and it puzzled him. Then he heard a rushing noise that puzzled him even more. He strained and stared.

"Oh, my God!" he suddenly shouted. He started toward the little bridge, yelling at the men in the cookhouse. "Get out! Get out of there! Get out!"

The rushing noise the cook had heard was now a loud roar as five hundred yards away, a mighty torrent of water roiled, tumbled, and cascaded down the mountainside, refilling the dry channel.

The wall of water rounded the final bend in the old riverbed, then rushed pell-mell toward the ranch buildings. It smashed into the granary, knocked in the walls, then continued on, sweeping away the wheat, oats, and corn that had been stored there.

By now, the roar of water was so loud that even the cowboys at breakfast could hear it, and a few managed to run out the door before the cookhouse, like the granary, was knocked off its foundation and swept downstream. There were several cowboys still trapped inside the cookhouse, and suddenly they found themselves fighting against the stove, table, and chairs that were being tossed around. Finally, they, too, managed to escape, dodging the swirling pieces of debris and swimming madly for dry land. Eventually, all of them made it to safety, though several of them lay on the ground, wet as drowned rats and gasping for breath.

Caulder had not been caught in the flood. He slept the night in the foreman's house, separate from the kitchen and from the big house. He had spent the entire day before looking for Slocum, puzzled by the fact that Slocum had now made an appearance. He knew that the incident with Mrs. MacTavish's hand, Dan, hadn't scared Slocum off, and he had told Draper that it wouldn't. However, Draper had insisted that it be done, and since Caulder was taking his money from Draper, he did what Draper ordered.

Though most wouldn't recognize it, Caulder did have a code of honor, and that code of honor dictated that if he took money for a job, he would do the job, even if he didn't see the sense of it. He had killed Dan, even though he hadn't seen the sense of it.

Since Slocum hadn't shown up on Crown Ranch land the day before, Caulder slept very little during the night. He had expected Slocum at any moment and he was alert to every sound and every movement all night long. As a result, he was still pretty groggy this morning, much too groggy to take breakfast with the men. If he didn't know better, he would almost believe Slocum had stayed away yesterday on purpose, knowing that Caulder wouldn't get a good night's sleep.

Caulder had gone over to the cookhouse a few minutes earlier to get a biscuit and a cup of coffee, which he took back with him. Then, when he heard the noise of the explosions, he groaned because he knew immediately what they were. Now he stood on the front porch of the big house and watched as the wreckage of the granary and cookhouse rolled and tumbled down the stream.

"What is it? What's going on?" Draper yelled as he rushed outside, pulling suspenders up over his shoulders. When he saw a river where moments before a dry bed had been, he cursed out loud. "Son of a bitch! Where did that come from?"

"It came from John Slocum," Caulder said.

"Slocum? How?" Draper sputtered.

"He blew the dams," Caulder explained.

"Goddamnit, Caulder, what is this? You said we could scare him off. He didn't even show up yesterday, did he? And yesterday was the deadline he set."

"You said we could scare him off, Draper," Caulder said. "I didn't."

"By God, who does he think he is? What does he think he's doing, blowing my dams like that?"

"He thinks he's declared war on us," Caulder said. "And I think he has."

"Oh, he has, has he? Well, I'll give that son of a bitch war. Get the men mounted," Draper ordered. "Get them mounted now and go out there after him. I want that son of a bitch's hide nailed to my barn door!"

"Don't you think it would be better if I went up by myself?" Caulder asked. "Or with just one or two of the men that I pick?"

"No, by God, I don't think it would be better!" Draper replied angrily. "You looked for him all day yesterday, didn't you? And did you find him? No, you didn't. I want Slocum to know who he's tangling with. And that means that I want every man who can ride, in the saddle looking for him."

"You aren't talking about the working cowboys are you? Don't you mean just the men I've hired?"

"No! I want the working cowboys, too. I want everybody, do you understand? I want that son of a bitch stopped and I want him stopped now."

"Mr. Draper, most of the working cowboys don't know one end of a gun from another. They aren't involved in this. They're just hands."

"Everybody!" Draper shouted. "Why is it so hard to make you understand? I want every man on this ranch mounted and after John Slocum!"

"Yes, sir," Caulder said, expressing by the tone of his voice that he believed Draper was making a mistake.

"Men!" Draper shouted to the cowboys who were still milling about and picking through the wreckage that had been deposited along the banks of the river. "I want John Slocum. Do you hear me? I want John Slocum! You bring him back to me, dead or alive, and it's worth five hundred dollars to every man here."

"Five hundred dollars to the one who catches him?" someone asked.

"No, by God! Five hundred dollars to every man here. Plus a bounty of one thousand dollars to the man who actually gets him."

"One thousand dollars?" one of the men asked, astounded by the figure.

"One thousand to the man who gets him," Draper said. "And five hundred dollars to everyone else."

"Yahoo! Let's go! Let's go get the bastard!" one of the cowboys shouted. All the men hurried to the barn to saddle up.

It took nearly ten minutes for all of them to get saddled and ready to ride. Finally, with many of them still dripping wet from their dunking in the river, they were ready to go. Caulder sat in front of them, a reluctant general to the small army.

"All right, men," Caulder said. "You know who we're after. Let's go get him."

"I've got the rope!" somebody shouted. "We'll hang the son of a bitch!"

Several of the others let out a yell and nearly two dozen horsemen started out at a gallop. Caulder went with them, but when he caught Barney's eyes, he shook his head in quiet frustration.

The riders galloped until their blood cooled, their enthusiasm waned, and their horses grew tired. Then one of them realized they were just running with no sense of direction or purpose. He pulled up, and because he was at the front of the pack, the others came to a halt with him.

"What is it? What's goin' on?" someone asked.

"Yeah, why did we stop?"

The rider who had caused the others to stop looked over at Caulder. "You're in charge of this chase, Sheriff. What do you think we ought to do now?" he asked. "I mean, we can't just go on a-runnin' around out here like chickens with our heads cut off, can we?"

"You finally figured that out, did you?" Caulder asked.

"Yeah," the cowboy answered sheepishly. He reached down and patted the neck of his horse. "I guess we did run off there half-cocked."

"Well, what now?" one of the others asked. "I mean, I ain' flatterin' myself that I'm the one who'll get the thousand dollars. But I ain't ready to just give up on that five hundred we'll all get if somebody else gets him."

"Does that mean you're ready to listen to me?" Caulder asked.

"Yeah, are you kiddin'? For five hundred dollars, we'll listen."

"All right then, we're goin' to divide up," Caulder said. "About three or four of you to a group. That way we can spread out and cover more territory."

"What do we do if we find him?" someone asked.

"If you find him and you kill him, you can divide the extra thousand among you," Caulder said simply.

"Yeah, yeah, that's for me," someone said. "I'm all for killin' the son of a bitch. That bastard nearly drowned me. And besides, he's worth just as much to us dead as he is alive."

Within a moment there were as many as five smaller groups, fanning out in all different directions. Now, with a sense of direction and purpose, their enthusiasm returned.

"Come on, Barney," Caulder said. "You, Tait, and Ely come with me."

"Where we goin'?"

"We're goin' back to the big house," Caulder said. "If Slocum is after MacTavish, that's where he's goin' to be headin'."

"What about these here other fellers?" Barney asked,

pointing to the men who were riding off on their own mission. "You just goin' to let them go off on their own?"

"Hell, yes, let the fools go," Caulder said. "We're better off rid of them."

14

John Slocum saw a little group of men coming after him. He was sitting calmly on top of a large, round rock, watching as four riders approached a narrow draw. The draw was so confined that they would not be able to get through without squeezing into a single file. It was a place that no one with any tactical sense would go. But these were not men with a sense of tactics. These were cowboys, fired up by the promise of a five-hundred-dollar reward for bringing in John Slocum, dead or alive. There wasn't a one of them who really intended to bring Slocum in alive. And there wasn't one of them who would balk at putting a noose around Slocum's neck. Because of that, they were men who could be easily lured into a trap.

Slocum stood up so he could clearly be seen against the skyline.

"Look! There he is!"

"He's up there!"

"Let's get him! Let's get the son of a bitch!"

The riders galloped through the draw, bent on capturing or killing John Slocum.

A couple of the men in front thought Slocum made an

easy target, so they pulled their pistols and began shooting up toward him as they rode. Slocum could see the flash of the gunshots, then the little puffs of dust as the bullets hit around him. The spent bullets whined as they ricocheted through the little draw, but none of the missiles came close enough to cause him to duck.

Slocum was smoking a cigar and now he leaned over, almost casually, to light two fuses. A little starburst of sparks started at each fuse, then ran sputtering and snapping along the length of fuse for several feet alongside the draw. The first explosion went off about fifty yards in front of the lead rider, a heavy, stomach-shaking thump that filled the draw with smoke and dust, then brought a ton of rocks crashing down to close the draw so that the riders couldn't get through.

The second explosion, somewhat less powerful, was located behind the riders. It, too, brought rocks crashing down into the draw behind them, closing the passage off. Slocum chuckled. It was going to be a long, slow process before the cowboys would be able to dig their way out of this.

Slocum scrambled down off the rock, then wriggled through a fissure that was just large enough to allow a man to pass through if he weren't riding. He had left his horse on the other side, and now he mounted and rode on, leaving the trapped cowboys behind him.

Slocum rode no more than a quarter of a mile before he saw the next group of riders. Attracted by the sounds of the explosions, they were hurrying over to see what it was.

"There he is!" someone shouted excitedly, pointing toward Slocum.

"Get him!" another yelled.

All four riders started after Slocum at a full gallop.

Slocum took his horse into a mesquite thicket. The limbs slapped painfully against his face and arms but they closed behind him, too, so that he was hidden from view. Slocum slowed his horse just enough to hop off, then he slapped him on the haunch, sending him on. Slocum squatted down behind a mesquite bush and waited.

In less than ten seconds, his pursuers came by. Slocum reached up and grabbed the fourth rider and jerked him off his horse. The man gave a short, startled cry as he was going down, but the cry was cut off when he broke his neck in the fall.

The rider just in front of that rider heard the cry and he looked around in time to see what was happening.

"Hey! He's back here!" he called. This rider had been riding with his pistol in his hand, so he was able to get off a shot at almost the same moment he yelled.

The man was either a much better shot than Slocum had anticipated or he was lucky, for the bullet grazed the fleshy part of Slocum's arm, not close enough to make a hole, but close enough to cut a deep, painful crease. The impact of the bullet, plus the effort of unseating the rider, caused Slocum to go down and he fell on his right side, thus preventing him from getting to his gun. The shooter had no such constraints, however, and he was able to get off a second shot. This time his bullet hit a mesquite limb right in front of Slocum's face, and would have hit Slocum had the limb not been there. Slocum knew then that the first shot had not been a lucky accident. This man could shoot.

Slocum rolled hard, not only to get out of the line of fire, but to be able to reach his gun. As he pulled it up in front of him, he saw that it was covered with dirt. He had a momentary concern that the barrel might be filled with dirt, and if so, it could explode on him when he pulled the trigger. Under the circumstances, however, he didn't have time to worry about that. He squeezed the trigger, heard the bang, felt the gun kick back in his hand, then saw the shooter grab his chest and pitch backward off his horse.

The other two riders, though they had initially answered the summons of their partner, suddenly realized that in the space of a few seconds, Slocum had cut the odds down to two to one. Those odds weren't to their liking, so they turned and galloped away.

Slocum borrowed one of the two riderless horses to recover his own. When he tracked his own mount down, he saw that one of the other Crown Ranch groups had already found it. They had dismounted and were giving their own animals a rest. One of the riders was taking a drink from a canteen, another was leaning up against a rock holding their horses, the third was examining Slocum's horse, while the fourth was standing a short distance away relieving himself. Slocum dismounted before they saw him and sneaked up closer to them on foot.

"It's got to be his horse," one of the men said. "It sure don't belong to Crown Ranch."

"How do you know?"

"It don't have a Crown Ranch brand."

"Hell, what's that mean?" one of the other men asked, laughing. "Half the animals on this ranch don't have the Crown Ranch brand."

"You sayin' Mr. Draper rustles?"

"Let's just say he throws a wide loop."

The others laughed.

"Hell, we all do," he went on. "Else we wouldn't be workin' here. Why do you think he pays us double what any other rancher would pay?"

"Turley, what the hell you doin' over there, anyways?" one of the cowboys asked.

"What's it look like I'm a-doin'?" Turley answered. "I'm waterin' the lilies."

"Goddamnit, you been pissin' for five minutes. At this

rate you could hire yourself out to them ranchers that can't get any water."

The others laughed.

"Why, didn't you see old Turley this mornin'?" one of the other men asked. "When he went in the river, he got as much water in him as on him."

"That's the pure truth of it," Turley said, returning to the others as he buttoned up his pants. "What do you say we backtrack this horse and try to find Slocum?"

"What do you think happened to him?"

"You heard all the shootin' a while ago," Turley said. "I figure he's wounded."

"Why do you say that?"

" 'Cause if he was dead, we'd know it by now. Whoever kilt him would be whoopin' and hollerin' to beat bloody hell, claimin' the extra thousand dollars. And if he wasn't wounded, we wouldn't have his horse."

"What are we going to do if we find him?"

"Do? Why, we're goin' to hang the son of a bitch, that's what we're going to do," Turley said with a smile. "That way we'll lay claim to the extra thousand."

"What if he's already wounded?"

"Especially if he's wounded," Turley said. "If we bring him in wounded, someone else is goin' to claim it was their shot done it and they'll be wantin' some of the money."

"Yeah, I guess you're right."

Suddenly, Slocum stepped out into the little clearing. His gun was already drawn.

"Where's Caulder?" he asked.

"Oh, shit!" Turley shouted, and he started for his pistol.

Slocum squeezed off a shot and a little mist of blood sprayed out from the side of Turley's head. Turley let out a yelp of pain and interrupted his draw to slap his hand against the source of his wound.

"You son of a bitch!" he shouted in pain and anger. "You shot off my ear!"

"You've got one left," Slocum said calmly. "I'll let you keep it if you answer my question. Where is Caulder?"

"I don't know," Turley grumbled.

Slocum cocked his pistol. "I might as well even you up," he said, pointing at Turley's other ear.

"No! No!" Turley shouted, holding both his hands out in front of him, showing the bloody palm of one of them. "I'd tell you if I knew, but I don't know where he went."

"Turley's tellin' the truth, Slocum," one of the other men said. "We broke up into different groups and we ain't seen Caulder since."

Slocum waited for a moment, then he eased the hammer back down on his pistol and lowered it.

"All right," he said with a sigh. "Take your guns out of the holsters and empty the loads onto the ground."

The men did as they were directed.

"You," Slocum said, pointing to the man nearest his horse. "Bring my horse over."

The man obliged and Slocum mounted, then looked at the other four horses.

"Let go of their reins," he ordered.

Again, Slocum's instructions were followed.

Slocum fired a couple of shots into the dirt near the horses. The animals reared up in fright and galloped off, their hooves clattering loudly on the rocky ground.

"Hey! What'd you do that for?" Turley asked. "It's a long walk back."

"It's going to be longer," Slocum said.

"What do you mean?"

"Take off your boots."

"What? Are you crazy? I ain't givin' you my boots," one of the men said.

"You can walk without boots, or crawl without feet," Slocum said dryly. "I don't give a damn which it is." He cocked his pistol again and aimed it at the feet of the man who had complained.

"No! Wait! Wait! We'll do it!"

"I thought you might," Slocum said.

All four men sat down then and began pulling off their boots. Slocum tossed a gunnysack to them.

"Put them in there and bring them to me," he ordered.

A moment later one of the men handed Slocum the sack of boots.

"Thanks," Slocum said. He hooked the sack over his saddle pommel and rode away, leaving the four cursing men behind him. He rode for at least two miles before he got rid of the boots.

A mile farther he found an irrigation canal and noticed that as a result of his blowing the dams earlier in the day this canal, which Draper had built to change the natural flow of water, was nearly dried up. There was, however, enough water for his purposes, so he dipped his kerchief into the stream and wet it so he could clean the wound in his arm.

A few minutes later, with the wound cleaned and bandaged, or at least bandaged as well as could be managed by using one hand, he remounted and rode off. He hoped to encounter Caulder out here. That would have made it easier for him when he went after MacTavish. But Caulder wasn't out here.

Seth Draper looked through the window of his study. In addition to the pistol in his holster, there was another on the desk behind him, loaded and easy to get to. He couldn't imagine Slocum getting through everyone to get to him but he wasn't going to take any chances. The son of a bitch had already gotten much further than he would have imagined.

The same thing could be said about Seth Draper. He had already gotten much further than anyone would have thought. Who could have believed that the scrawny orphan back in New York, living out of trash barrels and off petty thievery, would ever live in a house like this, owning land for as far as the eye could see, and running enough cattle to feed an army?

Draper had already come much further than anyone who was born in New York City's Hell's Kitchen had a right to expect, and most men in Draper's position would be satisfied with the wealth already amassed. But not Seth Draper. There was a hunger in Draper's gut that still ached from those days when he had to literally beg for a crust of bread.

Draper began his life of crime as a purse snatcher, burglar, and shoplifter. Then he graduated to armed robbery, but one of his jobs went bad and he killed someone. With the police looking for him, he left New York that same day, signing on to the crew of a sailing ship that was headed for San Francisco.

He was not a good sailor, and in addition to frequent lashings, he spent forty-three days of the one-hundred-twenty-day passage in the brig. Two days before they made San Francisco, the ship's chief bo'sun fell overboard. At least, that was how it was recorded in the ship's log. There were some who, correctly, suspected Draper pushed the bo'sun over the rail. After all, the bo'sun had been Draper's biggest adversary during the entire voyage. But as the ship's master explained, suspicions aren't evidence so he couldn't bring charges. He could, however, put Draper ashore in San Francisco, and that is exactly what he did.

Draper left the ship in San Francisco, tried prospecting and failed, then went back to his old ways of supporting himself by stealing from others. Then he got involved with some forgers and had some success in managing to put mining claims in enough dispute that the rightful owners would pay off, rather than fight it in court.

It was there that he first heard about Spanish land grants. He read an article about a huge amount of land in Texas that was turned over because of a claim verified by an old Spanish grant. Armed with this information, and the ability to get documents forged, Draper had only to await his opportunity.

That opportunity came when Ian MacTavish visited San Francisco. MacTavish married Emma Ritter, and though in the female-scarce world the loss of any woman, even a whore, was a major blow, most were happy for her because she had married not only a man she apparently loved, she had married a wealthy man. It was listening to a description of MacTavish's holdings that gave Draper the idea of where he would put his plan into action. Through his underground contacts, he found a judge who could be paid off, submitted his claim, and was rewarded with a sizable chunk of MacTavish's land. That was a good start, but he would never be satisfied until he owned every blade of grass and every cow in the valley. And that especially included Cross Pass Station.

He was already well into taking possession of the cattle belonging to Cross Pass. With a branding iron of one diagonal slash, it was a simple matter to change the brand from CP for Cross Pass, to CR for Crown Ranch. But rustling a few dozen, or even a few score head, at a time wasn't fast enough. He needed some way to take over Cross Pass. And of course, once he controlled Cross Pass, the other, smaller ranches would fall quickly.

Seth Draper pulled the drapes to, then decided to check on his prisoner. Going upstairs, he pulled the trapdoor down, lowered the ladder, then climbed up into the attic. To the degree that is was possible, MacTavish was sitting up on the bed, though as his legs were chained to the foot of the bed, he couldn't put them on the floor.

"What was all the noise?" MacTavish asked.

"Nothing."

"Nothing? It sounded like a cannon going off."

"Slocum blew the dam," Draper said. "The old dry beds are filled with water again. It took out the cookhouse and the granary and, no doubt, rerouted my entire irrigation system. In a matter of seconds the son of a bitch has destroyed what it took me years to build."

"It will be good to meet this man, Slocum," MacTavish said. "It's honored I will be, to shake his hand."

"You think I'm going to let you live that long?" Draper asked.

"Aye. You've got to keep me alive for your foul plan to work," MacTavish said. "So you'll nae do anything until the last minute. But 'tis my belief that you'll miscalculate and all this will be coming down on you."

Draper growled, then pulled his pistol and pointed it at MacTavish. He drew the hammer back.

"What's keeping me from killing you right now?" he asked.

"I can nae think of a thing," MacTavish said. "If you're of a mind to, go ahead. Pull the trigger."

"Are you crazy?" Draper said. "Your life is in my hands!"

"Laddie, I've lived my life ready to die for the last fifty years. I'm as ready now as I've even been, or ever will be. If you're going to kill me, do it and be done with it. Otherwise, go away. You are as annoying as a fly on dung heap."

The blood vessel in Draper's temple throbbed and he wanted to shoot MacTavish more than anything. But MacTavish was right. For his plan to work, Draper had to keep him alive. At least for now. He lowered the hammer, then put the pistol back in his holster.

"I'm going to let you live, for now," he said, pointing at MacTavish. "But when all this is over . . . when I don't need you anymore . . ." he let the sentence hang, threat-eningly.

There were several shots fired from outside, not too far from the house. Startled, Draper hurried over to look through the curtains.

"Sounds like he's getting closer," MacTavish said.

"I'd better go check on things," Draper said, starting toward the open trapdoor and the ladder that led to the lower floors.

"Draper?" MacTavish called.

"Yes?" Draper looked back toward him.

"Don't let the door hit you in the ass on your way out."

15

"It wasn't anything," Caulder said, answering Draper's query about the cause of the shooting. "Just some of the men shooting at ghosts, that's all."

"You're sure?"

"I'm sure."

Caulder was good at his job. He was also good at reading men, and he knew that John Slocum was a person who did what he set out to do. That meant that no matter where he was now, he was going to turn up here, at the big house. This is where MacTavish was, and MacTavish was Slocum's goal.

Though Draper had ordered everyone who could ride to go after Slocum, there were several cowboys who, for one reason or another, hadn't gone. Many were performing some task at another part of the ranch at the time and weren't even aware of what was going on until after the impromptu posse left.

Learning that Draper had offered a five-hundred-dollar bonus to be paid to everyone as soon as Slocum was caught, they were eager to be perceived as being part of the search, even though they were back at the ranch house.

When they thought they saw something moving, they opened fire, continuing until Caulder was able to get them to stop. That was the shooting Draper had heard.

"Have you got him?" Draper asked. "Have you caught the son of a bitch?"

"Not yet," Cauler replied.

"Then what the hell are you doing hanging around here? Why aren't you out looking for him?"

"We've got men combing the entire range," Caulder answered. "Maybe someone will get lucky. But the real place to look for him is right here."

"Right here? What do you mean?"

"I mean he's goin' to come here to get MacTavish," Caulder said. "And when he does, we'll get him."

"Surely he won't try it now that we're onto him, will he?" Draper asked. "I mean he'd be a fool to try it right under our noses. The only way we're going to find him is to go out after him. Now get back out there and find him."

"Mr. Draper, you hired me to take care of this kind of business for you, didn't you?" Caulder asked. "So that means you have to have some confidence that I can do it, or you wouldn't have hired me in the first place. Am I right?"

"I suppose so," Draper admitted.

"Then let me do my job. Otherwise, you can just pay me off, right now, and I'll be on my way."

Draper stared at the albino for a long moment, then sighed. "All right," he said. "We'll try it your way."

"That's more like it," Caulder said. "Now, you men, get rifles!" he ordered the others. "Get into your positions! Slocum is going to be comin' around sooner or later."

"What about the others?" one of the cowboys asked. "The ones that are still ridin' around out there."

"What about them?" Caulder asked.

"Well, shouldn't we send someone out there to bring them in?"

"What the hell for?" Caulder asked. "They'll just get in the way."

"But, what if they find Slocum?" one of the men asked. "Will we still get our bonuses? I mean, even though we aren't lookin' for him?"

"Mr. Draper said the five hundred dollars is for everyone," Caulder said. "That would include the men who are back here."

"Yeah, but there's a thousand dollars for the one that gets him," one of the cowboys complained. "I don't see anyone who stays here collectin' on that money."

"Then go join the others if you want to," Caulder said easily.

"Really? It's all right with you if I go out to look for him?"

"Sure," Caulder said. "And since Slocum is wandering around somewhere out there between us and them, who knows? You might get lucky and run across him yourself. You can take him, can't you? If you can, you won't even have to split the thousand dollars."

"Yeah, that's right isn't it?" the cowboy said with a broad grin. "Maybe I'll just . . . hey, wait a minute!" he said, suddenly realizing the implications of it. "There's no way I'm going to go up against Slocum by myself. What good is a thousand dollars if I'm dead? I'm not going out there."

"Does that mean you're staying here?"

"You damn right it does."

"Then you'll do what I tell you without giving me any more of your shit."

"Sure, Sheriff, whatever you say," the cowboy acquiesced meekly.

Caulder put the cowboy into one of the rifle pits, then he scattered the others out, putting them in defensive positions all around the big house. Once that was done, they waited. And they waited.

It was midafternoon and the sun was midway down in the western sky. The men were suffering from the heat and they slapped at flies and gnats and squinted into the unrelenting glare of bright sunlight as they waited. The longer they waited, the more nervous and irritable they became.

Slocum knew that a long afternoon of waiting would just increase the tension. That was one of the reasons he hadn't made any further moves once he got into position. Right now he was on a hill about two hundred yards away from the big house, and he had been there since before lunch. He knew when it was lunchtime, because the cook, who no longer had a cookhouse, had prepared his meal around the back of a chuck wagon. It was a hearty, appetizing meal and Slocum could smell the meat and potatoes from his position. His stomach growled in protest. All he had to satisfy his own hunger was a piece of jerky and a couple of swallows of water. He placated himself by remembering meals he had eaten in the past and by thinking of meals he would eat in the future. He had gone on jerky and water before, he could do it again.

After his meager meal, Slocum lay flat on his stomach, then looked through his binoculars at the activity below. He had known that he would find Caulder and a few of his gunmen here, but he was a little surprised by how many others were still around. He had thought that everyone would be out roaming all over the range country looking for him.

Though he was surprised at the number of defenders there were here at the ranch, he wasn't surprised by the preparations they had made for him. Caulder knew business and Slocum knew the defenses would be well laid out. From this position, however, Slocum was able to make a careful survey of the defensive positions Caulder had constructed. That knowledge would come in handy when he made his move.

There were four rifle pits around the plaza, each pit containing two men, with each man in the pits having an overlapping field of fire. The overlapping field of fire meant that there was no way to cross the plaza or approach the big house without coming under fire from one of the defenders.

In addition to the rifle pits, Slocum saw that Caulder had placed five more men in strategic locations. There was a man on the roof of the foreman's house, one on top of the barn, and another one in the hayloft. There was also a man at a window on the second floor and finally, a firing platform built high in the cottonwood tree that stood just by the northeast corner of the house. In addition to the rifle pits and the sharpshooters' positions, Slocum saw that there were at least two more men downstairs inside the front room of the big house.

Caulder and three of his riders didn't have any specific defensive position but were located to be able to move instantly to any place where they might be needed. Reluctantly, Slocum had to congratulate Caulder on constructing his defense. A good-sized army couldn't get through.

Ah, but that was the thing of it, Slocum thought. He wasn't an army, he was one man. And one man, sneaking through the cracks, might just be able to get through.

Slocum had seen Draper at lunchtime. He came out to the chuck wagon and spoke with several of the men, then went around and examined all the defensive positions. Shortly after lunch Draper disappeared back into the big house and Slocum hadn't seen him since.

Slocum took another look at all the windows of the big house. He saw the rifleman in the window of the top floor, then he swept his binoculars across the front, looking in through each window, until he came to the dormer window in the attic that was nearest to the cottonwood tree. What he found interesting about that window was the fact that the curtains there had a gap in the middle, as if someone had been looking through them. All the other dormer window curtains hung as straight as if they were sewn shut.

Slocum lowered the binoculars and smiled.

"I'd just about bet my whole bonus that that's where you are, MacTavish. You just stay put, and I'll come after you. I don't know if anyone has told you yet, but you are worth fifteen hundred dollars to me. One thousand five hundred dollars, just waiting there, waiting for me to walk in and pick it up."

Slocum chuckled quietly.

"Of course, there are a few obstacles I must get by."

As the sun dipped lower in the west, Slocum decided to try and improve his position. There was another protected spot off to his left, a little ridgeline that protruded, like a finger, pointing right at the big house. The end of the finger was a hundred yards closer than he was now, and from there, Slocum would be able to see more clearly what was going on. But if he was going to do it, he was going to have to do it now, before it got too dark to see. To reach it, however, he would have to cross an open area about fifty yards wide.

Slocum moved back down off the rock and walked over to his horse. Since he had gotten into position, his horse had enjoyed a fairly relaxed afternoon cropping grass. Slocum figured it should be well rested now, which was a good thing, because he had quite a task in front of him. Slocum was going to call upon him to run the gauntlet.

"You ready, horse?" Slocum asked, patting the horse on its neck. "I hope so, because when we go, you're going to have to give me all you've got."

Gripping his pistol, Slocum put his foot in the stirrup

and lifted himself up. But he didn't get in the saddle. Instead, he remained bent over, hidden behind his horse. Once he had his balance and a good hold, he urged the animal across the open area. He broke out into the clearing at a full gallop.

"There goes his horse!" someone shouted.

"Yeah, but where's he at?"

"Maybe his horse got away from him!"

"The hell it did! There the son of a bitch is, hangin' on to the other side!" someone else yelled. "Shoot him! Shoot the bastard!"

Knowing now that he had been spotted, Slocum raised up and fired across the top of his horse.

Those who were closest began shooting, and even after Slocum had made it all the way across and was completely out of their line of fire, they kept up their shooting until, finally, Caulder shouted at them to stop.

"Cease fire! Hold your fire, Goddamnit! Hold your fire! You're just wasting ammunition!"

The firing fell silent.

"Where'd he go?"

"Was he hit?"

"Does anyone see him?"

"Ever'one just keep your mouth shut and your eyes open!" Caulder ordered.

Slocum was in a good, secure position now. He was close enough to observe everything. Close enough even to overhear the men when they shouted at each other. Realistically, he knew this was as close as he was going to be able to get until it got dark. But with the sun already a bloodred disk low on the western horizon, he knew that darkness wasn't too far away.

Before it was too dark to see, Slocum made a careful examination of the big house. Once he saw Draper peering anxiously through the downstairs window. He would like to have seen MacTavish, just to reassure himself that he was in the house, and that he was still alive. He thought he knew where he was, but that was based only upon the information given him by Juanita.

Even if his information was correct, though, and MacTavish was in the attic, the question still remained, how was he going to get to him?

Slocum decided to wait until around twelve-thirty or one o'clock in the morning. He had made them wait all night, the night before so he knew that many of them had gone without sleep. He knew, also, that when someone tried to stay awake the whole night, they would be least alert just after midnight. If he was lucky, he might catch some of them napping.

Emma and Julie had moved out of the hotel and into the private car, though the car was still parked on the side track at the depot. They hadn't gone back out to the ranch because Emma didn't want to face being there without Ian. Also, any news of Ian would more than likely come back to town so she decided to wait it out right here in Prosperity.

She wished there was some way Slocum could get word back to her as to what was happening. It was frustrating to live in modern times, where through the miracle of telegraph one could have instant communication across thousands of miles, yet not be able to know what was going on no more than ten miles from here. Maybe someday someone would invent a type of pocket telegraph where, no matter where one was, they could send and receive messages. She knew that scientists were very clever, and no doubt that day would come. Until that time, however, one could only wait.

Manuel had offered to cook their meals in the car for them, but they declined, saying they would take their meals in the restaurant. That was really Julie's idea since she felt shut-in by spending too much time in the car. In fact, even though they had taken their supper at Manuel's Restaurant tonight, Julie was still feeling restless so, as Emma was having a second cup of coffee, Julie took a walk.

She had been gone no more than ten minutes when she returned with former sheriff Lane and another man. At first Emma felt a twinge of fear, thinking perhaps they had news, and the news wasn't good. But as she studied the expression on Julie's face as they approached the table, she knew that couldn't be the reason for the visit. She couldn't quite read Julie's face, but she knew that she wasn't seeing worry or sorrow as it would have been if the news was bad.

"Aunt Emma," Julie said, introducing the stranger. "This is Mr. Garrison."

Garrison was a short, rather rotund man with thinning blond hair and watery blue eyes. She was sure he wasn't from Prosperity, because she had never seen him before. Besides, he was wearing a three-piece suit, something only the bankers and lawyers of the town wore, and she knew all of them. In addition, Garrison was carrying a small grip.

"I'm Jerome Garrison, Mrs. MacTavish," Garrison said, extending his hand. "I'm with the United States Land Office, in Denver."

"You're a long way from home, Mr. Garrison," Emma said. "How can I help you?"

"It's not how you are going to help him, Aunt Emma," Julie said, rather excitedly. "It's how he is going to help you."

"Oh? And how is that?"

Garrison placed his grip on the table then opened it. "I have here . . . uh, do you mind if I sit down?"

"No, no, of course not," Emma replied. "Please forgive me for not offering you a chair before now."

"Thank you." Sitting down, Garrison began systematically removing papers from his grip. As he removed them he studied each of them closely, then spread them out on the table in what was obviously a specific pattern. Except for mumbling a few incoherent sentences to himself, he said nothing for a long time. Anxious as to what this was all about, Emma looked up at Julie.

"Wait," Julie said. "Just wait, you'll see." She was smiling broadly so Emma's anxiety went away, but not her curiosity.

Finally, Garrison quit moving the papers around. Then he took out a pair of glasses, put them on very carefully, and cleared his throat. It looked, at last, as if he was about to speak.

"No, wait," he said, moving two papers around.

Emma lost her patience. "For heaven's sake, Mr. Garrison, what is it?" she demanded.

"Ah, here we go," Garrison said, putting the last paper down. He looked up at Emma. "You are Mrs. MacTavish. Mrs. Ian MacTavish?"

"Yes, for crying out loud!"

"Then this information is for you. My research has turned up documents from the *Recopilacion de las Leyes de los Reynos de las Indias* that predates the claim filed by Mr. Seth Draper."

Emma shook her head. "I'm sorry," she said, "but I don't have any idea what you are talking about."

"Oh, I'm sorry," Garrison said. "It's the Spanish law of land allocation in America."

"Spanish land grants, Aunt Emma."

"Oh, those dreadful things," Emma said. "That's the way Draper stole land from us."

"Now, of course, I couldn't bring the original documents with me, but these are certified copies," Garrison continued. "Do you see these dates?" he asked, pointing to the documents. "Everything is in Spanish, but the year, 1764, is easy to see."

"Yes, I see that."

"As I said, these are certified copies of documents that have been previously validated as authentic Spanish land grants. Now, look at this date. What do you see?"

"It looks like 1773."

"Yes, ma'am. That's the date that was on the documents filed by Seth Draper."

"That's a later date," Emma said. "So, what does this mean?" She was beginning to see where this was going, but she wanted to hear it from the government's man.

"At first, we thought it just might be a question of disputed rights, that perhaps the later grant overturned the first grant," Garrison said. "But as we looked into it, we discovered that the grants submitted by Draper are completely invalid. Forgeries. Now, whether or not Draper knowingly filed forgeries . . ."

"Believe me, if they are forgeries, he knew it. He not only knew it, I've no doubt but that he arranged to have them done," Emma said.

"Yes, ma'am, well, that may be true, but if so, that comes under the Department of Justice, not the office of land management. I have nothing to do with bringing Mr. Draper to justice. I do, however, have the authority to inform you that the land Draper took by virtue of these documents, is hereby reverted to its original owner. That original owner, I believe, is Ian MacTavish."

"Isn't that wonderful Aunt Emma?"

"Yes," Emma said. "Although if the government won't enforce it, I don't expect Draper is going to give up the land that easily. Especially if all there is is a piece of paper."

"Mrs. MacTavish," Lane said. "If you will swear out a warrant for . . ." He looked at Garrison. "What was that called?"

"Unlawful tenure of private property," Garrison said.

"Yes, unlawful tenure of private property . . . you swear out that warrant and I'll serve it."

"You'll serve it? How can you serve it?"

Lane smiled. "I've got my old job back."

"What? Why, that's wonderful! But how did that happen?"

"Mr. Garrison went to the council with proof of fraud on the part of Caulder. When they saw that, even the ones who were for him in the beginning wanted him fired. So, the council voted him off, then hired me. I'd be glad to make serving this warrant my second official duty."

"Your second?"

Lane smiled. "My first official act was to fire Deputy Boyle."

Emma laughed. "Congratulations, Sheriff," Emma said. "And yes, I'll be glad to swear out the warrant. Though, in truth, I would rather wait and let Ian do it. I know it is something he will particularly enjoy."

"Then we'll wait," Lane promised.

16

It was about an hour after dark when Slocum got an unexpected break. The cowboys who had spent the day
searching the range for him were just now coming back
to the ranch. They were tired, hungry, and frustrated over
not yet having won the five-hundred-dollar bonus they
were promised. They rode boldly and irately right up to
the ranch. Unfortunately for them, they made no effort to
identify themselves. The men who were manning the ad-
vance rifle pits were already so nervous that they were
jumping at every shadow.

They had completely forgotten about those who were
out on the range and were totally surprised to see a large
body of men ride up on them.

It was too dark to see and the men were too edgy by
the circumstances to exercise caution. One of them put
into words what all of them thought.

"Oh, shit! Look at that!" one of the men in the rifle pit
shouted. "Slocum's got a whole army with him!"

A rifle shot ran out from one of the pits, and it was
returned by the approaching horsemen, who thought *they*
were being fired at by John Slocum. Their return shot was

answered by another and by another still, until soon, the entire valley rang with the crash and clatter of rifle and pistol fire.

The night was lit up by muzzle flashes, bullets whistled, whined, and plunged into horseflesh, or worse, buried themselves deep in the chest of one or more of the hapless cowboys.

Slocum realized at once what was happening. There was no need now to wait until after midnight. He could take advantage of the opportunity that was just presenting itself. As the guns banged and crashed around him, he sneaked out of his hiding position. He mounted, then rode north for a couple hundred yards, out of the line of fire. He had no intention of getting shot accidentally when none of them had been able to shoot him by design during the entire day.

From his new position the thump and rattle of gunfire was much quieter. Slocum looked back toward the battle and saw flashes of light from each gunshot. He began formulating his plans on just how to utilize this diversion to get into the house and find MacTavish.

The first thing he had to do was get down to the house unobserved and without risking a stray bullet. The revitalized riverbed, now filled with swiftly flowing water, gave him an idea. He saw a large tree limb lying close to the river's edge. The tree limb's bark had been stripped off by the wind and the wood underneath polished by the shifting sands and bleached white by the sun. Slocum dragged the limb over to the river, then, taking off his shirt, he wrapped his pistol belt, hat, and the three remaining sticks of dynamite in it, and tied it to the topmost branch. He pulled the limb out into the water and was gratified to see that his shirt and the shirt's contents remained dry.

The surge of the river was quite severe, however, and it nearly pulled the big limb away from him, but that was exactly what Slocum wanted. He grabbed hold of the back end of the limb, which effort increased the elevation of his little bundle, thus ensuring a dry passage, then dived forward, lifting his feet up from the river's sandy bottom. The limb, acting as a raft, supported him quite well and Slocum was swept along by the swift current downriver toward the house.

During the fighting the barn had caught fire and the men who had been shooting from the loft and the barn's roof had to abandon it. Now the burning barn cast an eerie, wavering orange glow over the entire scene, illumination enough to provide shadows as targets, but not bright enough to allow anyone to be identified and thus end the confusion.

The fire lit up the river, too, but no one saw the drifting tree limb, or if they saw it, they paid no attention to it. It was for certain that no one saw Slocum, because when he guided the limb to shore and retrieved his shirt, the gunfight was still going on.

Slocum climbed up the riverbank, then put his shirt and gun belt back on. Thrusting the three sticks of dynamite down into his shirt, he crouched over; then, running low, he darted up to the back of the house. He ducked through a portico, ran across the stone piazza, then slipped in through the back door.

By the ambient light of the burning barn, Slocum was able to pick his way through the downstairs part of the house. When he reached the parlor, he saw Draper. The rancher was standing just under the portrait of himself, a little behind the fireplace so that the stone façade provided him with some additional protection from the flying bullets. Slocum couldn't help but draw an unflattering comparison between the man who was cowering behind the fireplace and the heroic figure who was portrayed in the painting above the fireplace.

There were two other men in the parlor with Draper,

standing at the window, looking out at the fighting that was going on outside.

"What's going on out there, Taylor? Simmons? Can either one of you see anything?" Draper asked.

"Not a damned thing," Taylor answered. "Except the burning barn and the flashes of gunfire."

"Where did they all come from?" Draper asked. "Where did Slocum get all those men?"

"Beats the hell out of me," Simmons said. "I thought he was a loner."

"Where's Caulder?" Draper asked.

"He's out there somewhere."

"What's he doing out there?" Draper demanded. "He should be in here protecting me. That's what I pay him for."

"He is protecting you, Mr. Draper," Taylor said. "That's why he's out there."

"You two men, don't you go out there," Draper ordered. "You stay in here with me, do you hear me? You make sure nobody gets in here."

"Don't you worry none about that, Mr. Draper," Taylor said. "I got no intention of goin' out there."

At that moment a bullet crashed through the front window, whistled across the room, and buried itself in the wall on the opposite side.

"Holy shit! Did you see that?" Simmons asked.

"We better get down," Taylor said. "We could get our fool heads shot off just by standin' in front of the window like this."

As if to emphasize his statement, another bullet crashed through another window. Both men dropped to the floor, all the while keeping a sharp eye outside. Draper was already lying on the floor.

With all three of them lying on the floor and looking through the front windows, Slocum was able to move from the door of the back room, across the open area of

the parlor, to the foot of the stairs. At that point he would
be no more than ten feet away from Draper, but as there
were no lanterns inside the house, the only illumination
was the ambient light of the burning barn, and that left
enough shadows that Slocum felt his chances were pretty
good.

Slowly, cautiously, Slocum started up the stairs. The
first step creaked, and Slocum came to a dead stop.

"What was that?" Draper asked.

"What was what? I didn't hear nothin'," Simmons replied. "You hear anything, Taylor?"

"No," Taylor answered.

At that moment, part of the barn caved in with a loud,
creaking crash.

"I heard that," Taylor said.

"Yeah," Draper said. "That must've been what I heard,
too."

Slocum waited until all three were looking through the
windows again, and then he started up the stairs. Fortu-
nately, only the first step was loose, and he was able to
climb the rest of them without another sound.

When he reached the second floor he was confused for
a moment by not seeing another flight of stairs. Then he
saw a trapdoor in the ceiling just over the head of the
stairs. He reached up to pull it down, and saw a ladder.
Pulling the ladder down, he scrambled up to the attic.

Except for the light coming up through the trapdoor,
the attic was completely dark.

"Mr. MacTavish?" Slocum called quietly. "Ian Mac-
Tavish, I'm John Slocum, here to take you home."

"Look out, laddie!" Ian called, but it was too late. Slocum saw stars, then nothing.

When Slocum came to, there was a painful bump on the
back of his head, so severe that he almost felt as if his
eyes were crossed. The attic was no longer in darkness,

because light was coming in through the dormer windows.

"Damn," he said, gingerly rubbing the back of his head. "How long have I been out?"

"Long enough that I though ye might be dead," Ian said.

Slocum looked over at Ian, seeing for the first time the man he had come to rescue. He was a big man, with broad shoulders and powerful-looking arms. He was wearing a plaid shirt and denim trousers.

"I'm disappointed," Slocum said.

"Disappointed?"

"If I'm going to all this trouble to rescue you, the least you could do is be wearing your kilt."

Ian laughed heartily. "Bless you, boy," he said. "Sure'n that's the first good laugh I've been able to enjoy since these thievin' bastards brought me to this place. 'Tis lucky you are that you aren't seeing me in a sleeping gown, for that's how I was dressed when the scoundrels took me. They let me put on a shirt and pants at least."

Still rubbing the back of his head gingerly, Slocum moved over to the dormer window and looked outside. Below, he saw Caulder and Draper standing out on the patio, near the water spigot.

"It's daylight."

"Aye. Midmorning I make it."

Turning away from the window, Slocum patted his empty holster and frowned. Then he patted his shirt pocket, and smiled. "They took my gun, but at least I've still got the makin's."

"Lord, laddie, and is it so chained you are to tobacco that it's the first thing you check?"

"I like a good smoke," Slocum admitted. "But right now I'm more interested in these." He pulled out a packet of matches.

"Aye, matches might come in handy, all right."

"Especially with these," Slocum said. He pulled the three sticks of dynamite from inside his shirt.

"Good Lord!" Ian said. "There's enough dynamite there to bring the house crashing down."

"That's true," Slocum said. "Now, let's see what I can do about getting you loose."

Slocum moved over to the bed to examine the chains that bound Ian. They were held together by a large padlock. Then, looking around the attic, he saw a loose nail. He began working on the nail.

"Laddie, would you be for tellin' me what you're doin'?"

"Why did they leave me unchained?" Slocum asked, not answering the question but working the nail back and forth, back and forth, trying hard to free it.

"I guess they figured why bother?" Ian answered. "They thought you were either dead or about to die. And truth be told, laddie, I thought so as well. You were out for an awful long time."

"Yeah, well, I hope folks aren't too disappointed by my survival," Slocum said. Suddenly the nail popped free. "Ah, I've got it."

Carrying the nail back over to the chains that held Ian, he stuck the point of the nail into the padlock, wiggled it a few times, and the padlock popped open.

"I say, laddie, sure'n that's one hell of a trick!" Ian said, rubbing his wrists where the chains had rubbed the skin raw. "Where'd you learn how to do that?"

"It's just something I picked up," Slocum said. Again, he looked through the window. Draper, Caulder, and now three other men were gathered on the plaza. "Looks like they're planning something," he said.

"Yes, my execution," Ian said. "But they aren't going to kill me all at once. Instead, they are going to chop me up, piece by piece, a hand, a foot, an arm, and send those pieces to Emma until she breaks."

Without answering him, Slocum crossed the attic floor to the other side. Looking through the window, he saw two men, but they were in a rifle pit, looking away from the house.

"It's going to be easier than I thought," Slocum said. "Most of the guards are looking to see if anyone is trying to come in, they aren't looking this way."

"Ahh, that's good. I think," Ian said, coming over to look through the window over Slocum's shoulder.

Slocum started to raise the window.

"What are you planning?"

"We're going to climb out on the roof."

"We?" Ian replied. "We as in you and I?" Ian pointed to the roof, then sputtered. "Laddie, sure'n you're not thinkin' an old man like me can climb onto the roof now?"

"Sure you can," Slocum said. "It's not that steep. All you have to do is keep your weight balanced."

Ian looked out the window. "Aye, keep my weight balanced," he said. "Still, I'm not as agile as I once was."

"You can do it," Slocum insisted. "You go first."

"Are you sure you want me first?" Ian asked. "What if I get out there, then can't move for the fear of fallin'? It might hold you up."

"No, it won't. I'll just give you a good kick in the ass," Slocum said.

Again, Ian laughed. "You're all right, boy," he said. "Slocum, you say? You sure that's not MacSlocum?"

"Come on, let's go."

Ian went through the window first, then carefully crawled out onto the roof. Balancing his weight as Slocum suggested, he moved far enough away from the window to allow Slocum to exit as well.

Slocum exited the window almost as easily as if he was walking through a door. He came up alongside Ian.

"All right, we're here. What do we do now?" Ian asked, overcompensating in order not to slide down the pitch of the roof.

"Now we have some diversion," Slocum said. "Wait here."

"Don't worry, I'll nae be going anywhere."

Slocum scurried across the roof as easily as a squirrel, then, reaching the chimney, he stood up and pulled two sticks of dynamite from inside his shirt. One of the fuses he pulled out, slightly, making it longer. The other fuse he bit off, making it only about one-fourth as long as the first. Then he lit both of them, dropped the one with the long fuse down the chimney and tossed the other over the edge of the roof, down to the plaza, in the general direction of Draper, Caulder, and the others. Then he lay down just on the reverse side of the peak of the roof and looked over so he could gauge the results of his action. The smoking, sputtering stick of dynamite described an arc through the sky, hit just on the edge of the plaza, about thirty yards away from the little group of men, then exploded, almost instantly. When it went off, it sent shards of stone scattering in all directions.

Although the bursting radius wasn't great enough to harm the little group, they were peppered with little shards of stone.

"Holy shit!" Caulder shouted. "What was that?"

"Into the house!" Draper yelled, running toward the front door. The others were right behind him, and they barely reached the front door when the other stick of dynamite went off, this one exploding from the fireplace. This explosion was so great that it blew out the bottom half of the chimney, along with a sizable portion of the house.

"Think you can climb down a tree?" Slocum asked, pointing to the top of the cottonwood where, earlier, Caulder had posted a rifleman.

"We're about to find out," Ian said, moving toward the side of the house. A large limb reached out to the roof, providing and easy path to the trunk of the tree. Once the men reached the trunk of the tree, it was fairly easy to climb down to the place where the lookout's platform had been, then much easier from there to the ground, because steps had been nailed to the tree.

The two men made it to the ground, then Slocum lit the last stick of dynamite and tossed it toward the front of the house. When this stick went off, half the front wall caved in.

"Down! Everyone down!" someone shouted from inside the house. "They've called out the army on us, and they're using cannons!"

The last stick of dynamite had caught the house afire and it, plus the fact that Draper was now convinced they were under an artillery attack, kept the Crown Ranch hands off guard. As a result, Slocum and Ian were able to make it to the corral unseen. Because the barn had burned last night, all the horses were now in the corral, including those that had previously been kept in stalls. The saddles that had not been left to burn in the tack room were also out in the corral, thrown across the top rail of the fence.

Slocum's horse was with the others, but he didn't have to worry about finding a saddle because although they had caught and corralled the horse, they hadn't bothered to unsaddle it. Ordinarily that would have angered him, but now it seemed like a lucky break. Especially since the rifle was still in the boot. If not for the rifle, Slocum would be unarmed.

"Grab a saddle and a horse," Slocum said.

"I don't see my saddle," Ian complained. "Don't be so damn choosy," Slocum said, grabbing the first saddle he saw and throwing it on the back of the first horse. Quicker than he would have thought possible, he had the horse saddled, then he handed the reins to Ian. "Get mounted— let's get out of here."

Slowly, quietly, they slipped away.

17

They rode for the rest of the day in heat so fierce that what little wind did stir blew against their faces like a breath from the mouth of a furnace. The land unfolded before them in an endless vista of rocks, dirt, cactus, and mesquite. The sun heated the ground, sending up undulating waves, which caused near objects to shimmer and nonexistent lakes to appear tantalizingly in the distance.

Normally it was one hard day's ride from Crown Ranch to Prosperity. It would be longer now, because Slocum wasn't going by the most direct route. He was taking a circuitous path because he hoped to avoid an ambush. That proved to be a vain hope, however, when a pistol cracked and a bullet whizzed by, taking his hat off, fluffing his hair, and sending shivers down his spine.

"Get down!" he shouted at Ian, but his warning wasn't necessary because Ian was off his horse as quickly as Slocum. Slapping their horses on the flank to get them out of the line of fire, the two men dived for the protection of a little outcropping of rocks, even as a second shot came so close that Slocum could hear the air pop as the bullet sped by.

Slocum wriggled his body to the end of the little bank of rocks, then peered around cautiously. Though he couldn't see anybody, he did see a little puff of smoke drifting north on a hot breath of air. That meant the shooter was somewhat to the south, so he moved his eyes in that direction. He saw the tip of a hat rising slowly above the rocks and he figured the shooter was raising up to take another shot.

Slocum watched as the hat began to move up, and he jacked a round into the chamber of the Winchester and waited. When enough of the hat was visible to provide a good target, Slocum aimed and fired. The hat sailed away.

"Ha! That's an old trick, Slocum," a voice called. "I had my hat on the end of a stick."

Slocum fired again, this time at the sound of the voice. His bullet sent chips of rock flying and he was rewarded with a yelp of pain.

"You son of a bitch! You sprayed rock into my face!" the shooter said.

"Sorry. I was trying to hit you between the eyes."

"Hold it!" a voice suddenly yelled behind Slocum, and when he turned, quickly, he saw someone standing behind Ian, holding a gun on Ian. "Duke, I've got 'em!" the man yelled. "You can come on in."

"Good job, Lee," the shooter named Duke replied. Duke stood up from his position behind a rock about thirty yards away from Slocum. "Well, looks like we're going to get ourselves that thousand-dollar reward."

"Maybe more, since we caught both of 'em," Lee said.

Duke started toward them, and because Lee had his gun pointed at Ian, Duke let his own pistol hang loose by his side.

Slocum was watching Duke approach when, from behind him he heard a strange grunt. "What the hell?" Duke shouted and, from the expression in Duke's eyes, he knew that, somehow, Lee had lost his advantage.

It took Duke a split second to realize that he had gone from being in command of the situation to being in danger. During that split second he decided that he had better bring his pistol up to firing position, but he made that decision too late, for Slocum already had a shell in the chamber of the rifle. Firing from the waist, he put a bullet exactly where he had told Duke he wanted to put the first one . . . right between Duke's eyes.

Cocking his rifle, he spun around to see what was going on behind him, but saw that a second shot wasn't needed. Ian had smashed his elbow into Lee's face, then, grabbing him, broke his neck with one quick jerk. Lee lay on the ground as dead as Duke.

"You all right?" Slocum asked.

"Aye."

Slocum walked over to look down at Lee, then he whistled. "Remind me never to get you pissed off," he said. "Better get his pistol," he added as he walked back over to get Duke's pistol for himself.

The night creatures raised their songs to the stars as Slocum and Ian MacTavish approached Prosperity. A cloud passed over the moon, then moved away, bathing the little town that rose up from the prairie in silver before them. Some of the buildings were dark, though most showed varying degrees of illumination, from the dull glow of a single lantern or candle to the brightness created by dozens of lamps. The most brightly lit buildings were the saloons.

Like the creatures of the prairie, the town dwellers had their own brand of night music. As Slocum approached the little community he could hear the orchestral change. The soft hoot of owls, the trilling songs of frogs, and the distant howl of coyotes gave way to tinkling pianos, off-key singing, clinking glasses, and an occasional outburst of laughter.

Slocum looked toward the depot and saw that Emma's private car was still sitting on the side track. Like the saloons, it was brightly lit.

The two men were about to move toward the car when a shadow passed in front of one of the car windows. That meant there were people outside, around the car.

"Hold it," Slocum said. "Someone's watching the car."

Slocum was pretty sure that Draper and his men were already in town. He wasn't surprised that they were here before him. As soon as they discovered that both Slocum and Ian were missing, they would have come to town. And they had the advantage of being able to come straight in, whereas it had been necessary for Slocum and Ian to come by a more circuitous route in order to evade recapture.

"I'm sure those are Crown Ranch riders down there," Slocum said. "There are at least four of them."

There was a sudden peal of laughter from the Red Bull. "Damn, that's Bodine," Ian said. "I recognize his hellish laugh."

"We've got to go somewhere to get off the street," Slocum said.

"What about Manuel's?" Ian suggested.

"Manuel's, yes, that's good."

The two men rode to Manuel's Restaurant, not by the street, but up the alley. Dismounting behind Manuel's, they knocked on the door of the kitchen. It was Juanita who let them in.

"Señor Slocum!" she said. Then, seeing Ian, her face broke into a big smile. "Señor MacTavish, you are alive!"

"I won't be much longer if I don't get something to eat," Ian said. "Whatever Manuel's cooking, it smells delicious."

"Here, sit over here," Juanita said, showing them a table in the corner of the kitchen. "I will tell Manuel you are here."

Manuel was out front but he came back to the kitchen quickly. Even as Juanita was preparing plates for Slocum and Ian, Manuel was standing by their table, warning them not to come out front because there were several Crown Ranch riders present.

"Is Draper in town?" Slocum asked.

"*Sí*, he is in town."

"And Caulder?"

"*Sí*, the Widow Maker. He is in town, too. They are here to kill you, I think."

"They are here to try," Slocum said. "But they aren't going to get the job done. Not if you help us."

"*Sí*, I will help you," Manuel said. "I am not very good with guns, but I will fight for you."

"No, it's nothing like that," Slocum said. "Do you know the boy who works at Heckemeyer's Auction Barn? His name is Timmy, I believe."

"*Sí*, Timmy Norton. He is a good boy."

"Find him," Slocum said. "Find him and bring him here, to the kitchen. Tell him I need him."

"Very well, señor, I will find him for you," Manuel promised. Pointing to some spicy beef, he told one of his cooks to give generous portions of it to the two gringos who were at the kitchen table. Then he pushed through the swinging door and disappeared into the front of the restaurant.

"Manuel, more tortillas!" Slocum heard someone shout from out front.

"And tequila. Much more tequila," another said, and his order was followed by laughter.

It was no more than five minutes later when Manuel and Timmy came in through the back door. Timmy hurried over to the table where Slocum and Ian were still eating.

"Mr. MacTavish, it's good to see you again," Timmy said.

"Thanks, laddie. How is my wife?" Ian asked.

"She is fine. They're keeping her and Miss MacTavish prisoner in the railcar. They won't let them out, and they won't let anyone else in to see them."

"The bastards," Ian swore.

"Mr. Slocum, all of Draper's men are saying you'll be shot dead the moment you set foot in town," Timmy said. "I'm glad to see you've made a liar out of them."

"Well, so far so good," Slocum replied. "How many of them are in town, do you have any idea?"

"No, sir. But there's a lot of them, that's for sure."

"Are they all together?"

"No, sir, they ain't. Caulder, he's down to the depot keepin' a close eye on Mrs. MacTavish. And Draper, well, he's got him that private apartment over the leather goods store." Timmy chuckled. "I reckon he's going to have to live there for a while. They're tellin' you left the ranch lookin' like Atlanta after the siege."

"They'll bloody well know he's been there," MacTavish said.

Timmy laughed again, then he grew curious. "Manuel said you needed my help. What can I do for you?"

"I need to get Mr. MacTavish down to the railcar. After that, I need to get it hooked onto an engine so I can get these good people safely out of town. Will you help us?"

"Mr. Slocum, there's no doubt in my mind but that you're the best man in this town. But even with my helpin' you, there would still be only two of us. And there's a whole army of them Crown Ranch riders, every one of them wantin' to get their hands on that reward money. No, sir, I don't see no way on God's green earth we're goin' to make it down to the depot."

"We're going to do it by evening the odds a bit," Slocum said.

"How we going to do that?"

"By using Draper. You say he is staying in an apartment over the leather goods store?"

"Yes, sir."

"Is he alone?"

"No, sir. There's a couple of men with him. Simmons and Taylor, I think."

Slocum recalled that they were the two men who had stayed close to Draper back at the ranch. "Yeah, I know who they are. We need to get Simmons and Taylor away from him."

"How?"

Slocum looked over toward the stove where Juanita was making more tortillas. Using the back of her hand, she brushed her hair back from her forehead. The motion accented her breasts and the curve of her hips. He smiled.

"You're going to be a procurer," he said.

"A what? What's that?"

"That's someone that drums up business for a whore."

"That won't work. All the whores are over in the saloon," Timmy said. "And right now they're being kept pretty busy."

"Then we'll just have to get us a new whore," Slocum said, still looking at Juanita.

"You want me to be a *puta*?" Juanita asked in a horrified voice, when Slocum told her his plan. She shook her head. "No, señor. I think you are a very good man, but I cannot do this thing. Not even for you."

Slocum shook his head. "You aren't actually going to do it," he said. "All you are going to do is stand out on the street in front of the leather goods store. Throw your hip out, pull up your skirt, put on a little show."

"I would be very embarrassed."

"You needn't be. You will be so far away that they won't see you clearly. Which is a good thing because some of them might recognize you from the ranch."

"Sure'n of the lassie does her job well, they'll nae be

lookin' at her face," Ian said, and they all laughed.

"Timmy will tell them where they can meet you. But it won't be real. Manuel, do you know a place we can send them . . . then keep them there for the rest of the night?"

Manuel smiled. "*Sí*, señor, I have many friends who will be *muy* happy to do that."

"Good. That will take care of them. I'll take care of Draper."

"We'll take care of him," Ian said.

"We need him alive," Slocum warned. "At least for the time being."

"Aye," Ian replied. "At least for the time being."

"Now, our only problem is how we get over there to get him, without being seen and recognized."

"I can send a couple of my friends," Manuel suggested. "Gringos pay no attention to Mexicanos."

"We might do that," Slocum said. He paused for a moment, then smiled. "On the other hand, we might become Mexicanos ourselves."

Wearing sombrero and serape, Slocum and Ian stood in the shadows in front of Manuel's Restaurant and watched as their plan unfolded. First Juanita stepped under a lamp-post and struck as provocative a pose as she could, then Timmy went across the street and up the side stairs that led to the apartment over the leather goods store.

"Yeah?" Simmons said gruffly, opening the door. "Wait a minute, I know you. You work at the stable, don't you?"

"I did. I'm in another business now," Timmy said.

"Yeah? Well, what does that have to do with me?"

"Would you look down in the street, sir?" Timmy asked.

"What the hell for?"

"Because I represent a certain young woman who

would like to sell her charms, if you know what I mean."
He pointed to Juanita.

On cue, Juanita exhibited her charms.

"Damn," Simmons said. "Would you look at that!"

"Are you interested?"

"Hell, yes, I'm interested. How much?"

"Three dollars."

"Three dollars? There's not a whore in town you can't
get for two dollars."

"Yes, but this girl is more beautiful than any other
whore in town."

"Sonny, one thing you got to learn about this whorin'
business is that all cats look gray in the dark," Simmons
said. He started to turn away.

"Wait!" Timmy said. "You're about to miss the best
part. For three dollars, you can bring a friend."

"Damn!" Simmons said, now showing definite interest.
"You mean she'll do two at the same time?"

"Yes. And if you share the cost, that will only be a
dollar and a half. That makes her cheaper than any other
whore in town," Timmy said.

"Taylor, come on! We've got to try this!"

"I'm with you," Taylor said. Like Simmons, Taylor had
looked down in the street to see what was being offered.

"Hold it!" Draper called. Draper had been sitting at a
card table playing solitare during the entire conversation.
He had paid no attention to it, until he realized that his
bodyguards were about to leave. "Where you boys goin'?"

"We're goin' to get a piece of ass," Simmons said.

"Both of you?"

"Yeah."

"Yeah, well . . . don't be gone too long. I don't trust
Slocum."

"Don't worry, this ain't goin' to take too long," Simmons promised.

After Timmy left, leading Simmons and Taylor on a

wild-goose chase, Slocum and Ian hurried up the same stairs. When the reached the top of the stairs, Slocum pushed the door open.

Draper was sitting at the card table with his back to the door.

"Did you forget something?" he asked.

"Yeah, I forgot to do this," Ian said.

"Wha—?" That was as far as Draper got before Ian laid him out with a hard, straight punch to the mouth.

With Draper out on the floor of his little apartment, Slocum and Ian wrapped him up in a blanket, then tied a sombrero on his head. Ian picked him up and tossed him over his shoulder, carrying him, like a sack of flour, back to Manuel's place.

"Hey!" a drunken Crown Ranch rider yelled, when they reached the street. Slocum put his hand on the butt of his pistol.

"If you Mex fellas can't hold your liquor, you ought not to be drinkin'," the Crown Ranch rider continued. He laughed at his own joke.

18

A rooster crowed.

Somewhere a back door opened, and a housewife came outside, carrying a bucket. She put the bucket under the spout and began pumping water. The squeaking clank, clank, clank of the pump could be heard all over town.

A dog barked.

A baby cried.

James Caulder had spent the night at the depot, and when the morning sounds woke him up, he stood, stretched, scratched, and looked out at the red disk of the sun, low in the eastern sky. He walked outside and peed on the railroad tracks, making no attempt to preserve modesty.

"Tull? Bodine?" he called as he buttoned up his pants.

Bodine had been sleeping on another bench in the depot, and at Caulder's call, he got up. Tull was walking down the street toward the depot, coming from downtown. He was carrying something, and when he got close enough, Caulder could see that it was a plate of biscuits and bacon. Caulder reached for one.

"You two fellas decide to sleep in this mornin'?" Tull

teased. "I already been all over town. Got these down at Manuel's."

"Anybody see any sign of Slocum or MacTavish last night?" Caulder asked, taking a big bite.

"Not hide nor hair," Tull answered. "There is somethin' strange goin' on, though."

"Strange? What do you mean, strange?"

"Well, it's Mr. Draper. Don't nobody seem to know where'bouts he is."

"He's in his apartment over the leather goods store," Caulder said. "Simmons and Taylor is with 'im."

"No, he ain't there. Simmons and Taylor ain't there neither, I done checked. He ain't at none of the cafés or the saloon, neither."

"What do you mean, Goddamnit? He has to be somewhere. What's the name of the guy that owns the leather goods store? Bradley? Did you check with him?"

"Yeah, I did, but he don't know nothin' about it, neither."

At the other end of town from the depot where Caulder, Bodine, and Tull were having their breakfast, Slocum and Ian were having their own breakfast back in Manuel's kitchen. Draper had spent the night in the kitchen with them, bound and gagged. Slocum walked over to him.

Smiling at him, he said in a quiet, conversational voice, "I'm going to take the gag off. But if you yell, I'm going to kick your teeth down your throat. Now, do you understand that?"

His eyes wide with fear, Draper nodded yes.

"And you'll be a good boy?"

Again, Draper nodded yes.

Slocum removed the gag. "Do you want breakfast?" Slocum asked.

"No. Would you mind telling me how long you are going to keep me here?"

"I'm going to keep you here long enough for Ian, Emma, and Julie to get out of town."

"And how are they going to do that?"

"Simple. We'll send a telegram over to Risco, asking the switch engine to come pick up their car. It should be here by this afternoon."

"You aren't going to make it. I've got forty men spread around town, all of them waiting for a chance at that one thousand dollars. Besides that, Caulder and some others are down at the depot. You'll never make it."

"If we don't make it, you won't make it," Slocum said.

"What do you mean by that?"

"When we move down the street toward the depot, I'm going to be holding a double-barreled shotgun right under your chin. I'll have the triggers tied back, and I'll be holding the hammers back with my thumb. If something was to happen to me, for example, say I was to get shot, then my thumb would just naturally let go and the hammers would snap shut, firing the gun."

"You're crazy."

"Yeah, people are always telling me that."

"Señor Slocum!" Manuel said, coming quickly into the kitchen.

"I think maybe you should come."

"What is it?"

"Come, *por favor.*"

Slocum, Ian, and Draper followed Manuel through the door back into the dining room of the café. Although there were several plates of half-eaten breakfasts on the tables, the room was completely empty. When Slocum reached the front of the café, he looked outside and saw that the street was also empty. That was strange, for this was the middle of the morning and the street should have been full of its daily commerce.

"Over there, señor," Manuel said, pointing across the street.

Looking in the direction Manuel pointed, Slocum saw
Caulder and Bodine standing on the front porch of the
leather goods store. A more thorough perusal showed him
that the street wasn't empty as he had thought, but was
lined with gunmen, crouched behind watering troughs,
standing behind the corners of buildings, behind wagons,
and several other places, all with their guns trained on
Manuel's café.

"Damn," Slocum said. "How'd they find out where we
were?"

Behind him, Draper chuckled. "I told you you wouldn't
make it."

"Slocum! Slocum, we need to talk!" Caulder shouted.

"All right," Slocum replied, shouting back through the
door. "Let's talk."

"We've got a friend of yours," Caulder said. Giving a
signal to someone, two men appeared from around the
corner of the bank. One of the two was Timmy Norton.
Timmy's face was badly bruised and bloodied, his hair
matted, and his clothes torn.

"Recognize this boy?"

"Yes."

"He was real helpful," Caulder said. "He told us where
to find you."

"I'm sorry, Mr. Slocum," Timmy said. "They beat it
out of me."

"Don't worry about it, son," Slocum said. "You've
been a friend. Caulder, what do you aim to do with him?"

"Oh, I think I'll just show this town what it means to
be your friend," Caulder said.

"Let the boy go," Slocum said.

"Sure, I'll let the boy go. Let him go, Bodine."

Bodine let Timmy go, then stepped back behind the
corner of the bank, while Timmy stood there for a moment, looking around as if unable to believe he had been
released.

"Come toward me, Timmy," Slocum shouted.

"Yeah, boy. Go toward him," Caulder said. Caulder and Bodine also slipped back out of sight.

Slocum didn't like this. He had a sick feeling in the pit of his stomach. Why did everyone on the street suddenly get behind cover. The hair stood up on the back of his neck.

Timmy didn't have the same sense of trepidation, and, smiling, he started toward Manuel's café. It looked as if everything would be all right, but when he reached the middle of the street, Bodine suddenly stepped around the corner of the bank and fired, hitting Timmy in the back.

"No!" Slocum shouted. "Bodine, you son of a bitch! I'm going to kill you!"

Timmy fell, facedown, in the dirt. From the way he was lying, Slocum knew he was dead.

"I hope all you good people of Prosperity saw that," Caulder shouted. "You good people who are hiding in your houses, under your beds, behind your women's skirts. I hope you saw what happens to people who don't know who their real friends are."

"Caulder! Caulder, get me out of here!" Draper shouted.

"Don't you worry none, Mr. Draper," Caulder replied. "We're goin' to get you out of there. Slocum, you got anything to say?"

Slocum had been keeping his eyes on the corner of the building where Bodine had gone. He knew that Bodine would eventually take a peek around the corner, and when he did, he was going to be ready for him. He rested his forearm on the windowsill to help steady his pistol, and he waited.

"Come on, Slocum, what do you say?" Caulder said again. "Why don't you be sensible and turn Draper and MacTavish over to us? If you do that, we'll let you ride out of town."

"You don't expect me to believe that, do you?" Slocum called back.

"Believe what?"

"That you would just let me ride out of town?"

Caulder laughed. "Well, I guess you got that all figured out, haven't you? No, the truth is, I'm afraid it's too late for that. I'm afraid it's going to have to end for you, right here."

"How about facing me down?" Slocum called. "Just you and me?"

"You'd like that, wouldn't you?" Caulder shouted back.

"I'm not the only one who would like it," Slocum said. "you know yourself, ever since I arrived, the whole town has been trying to get us together. What do you say? You want to do it?"

All the while Slocum was talking, he was keeping his eye on the corner of the building where he had seen Bodine go. Then his vigil was rewarded. Slocum saw the brim of a hat appear, then a part of the crown, and finally a sliver of face. Slocum cocked his pistol, aimed, took a breath, and let half of it out. He waited until the head was far enough around the corner for Bodine to take a look at what was going on. When the Bodine's eye appeared, Slocum touched the trigger. His pistol barked and Bodine spun around, then fell into the alley with a bullet hole just above his eye.

"Jesus, Caulder! Did you see that?" another voice shouted. "How did he do that?"

"Take it easy," Cauder said. "Bodine got a little careless, that's all.

"I'm gettin' out of here!" someone shouted.

Slocum saw the flash of a pistol shot, and a bullet came crashing through the window of the café. Looking outside, Slocum saw that a Crown Ranch rider had left his hiding place and was making a mad dash across the street to get to another position. A the cowboy ran, he continued to fire toward the café.

Slocum fired back once. His bullet caught the cowboy high in the chest, and he pitched forward, halfway across the street, ironically falling across Timmy's body.

There were two people on the roof of the bank across the street and they both fired at Slocum. Slocum returned fire. One of the shooters pitched forward clutching his stomach. He tumbled off the roof. Slocum missed the second shooter, but his shot was close enough to send the man scurrying for cover.

"Draper," Slocum said. "Tell them to quit shooting."

Another volley of bullets came crashing through the windows of the café. By now all the glass was gone, but the bullets whipped through the curtains, smashed into the tables and crockery, and slammed into the wall on the opposite side of the room.

"Quit shooting," Draper called.

"I don't think they heard you."

"I said quit shooting!" Draper called again.

"That's no good," Slocum said. "They can't hear you. Get up front, near the window."

"What?"

"Do it!" Slocum ordered.

Sweating and shaking in fear, Draper walked to the front window.

"My God! Are you crazy?" Draper shouted in terror. "Caulder! Quit shooting! For God's sake, quit shooting!"

"Hold your fire, men, hold your fire!" Caulder ordered. "Mr. Draper, are you all right?"

"Yes," Draper said. "But I won't be, if you don't stop this."

"All right, Mr. Draper, whatever you say," Caulder replied. "We'll find some other way to get you out of there."

With the gunfire temporarily silenced, Slocum heard the

sound of a distant train whistle. He picked up the shotgun and shoved it under Draper's chin.

"What are you doing?" Draper asked.

"Hear the train?" Slocum replied. "What do you say we go down to the depot and meet it?"

19

"If there is anyone waiting out there, don't shoot!" Draper yelled from the front door of Manuel's. "For God's sake, don't shoot!"

"All right, let's go," Slocum said, shoving the double barrels of the shotgun under Draper's chin.

Draper led the way out into the street, his head held rigidly erect by the shotgun, his eyes open wide in fear. Slocum was right behind him, holding on to him with his left hand while with his right he held the shotgun. Ian was just behind Slocum.

Slocum saw movement behind the corner of the leather goods store.

"I don't know who's over there," Slocum shouted. "But I want to tell you that my thumb is already getting tired."

"Come out!" Draper shouted. "Come out in the street so he can see you!"

Two men walked out then, both of them carrying guns.

"Throw the guns down and put your hands up," Slocum ordered.

The two men did as ordered, then walked on either side of him as a human shield against anyone who might take a shot.

Slocum shepherded his little party toward the depot. The train whistle they heard a moment ago was now much closer, and in fact, not only the whistle could be heard, but the chugging, puffing sound of the engine as well.

Manuel's was at one end of the street, the depot was at the other. About one hundred yards separated the two structures. As Slocum looked down the one hundred yards, he could see the Crown Ranch riders, some of them on the roofs behind the false fronts of the buildings, some of them just inside doorways, others near the corners of the buildings. At the far end of the street he could see the MacTavish private car, and standing on the depot platform in front of the car were Emma and Julie.

"Ian!" Emma shouted excitedly. She started toward them.

"Ian, tell her to stay until we get there," Slocum said.

"Emma, no, get back!" Ian said, waving at her. "Get back!"

Understanding, Emma nodded her head, then got back onto the platform to wait.

"Good," Slocum said. "Getting her out in the middle of the street now would just complicate things. It's easier if she stays there."

"It doesn't make any difference what she does, Slocum," Draper said. "You won't make it alive to the other end of this street."

"You damn well better hope I do," Slocum said, jamming the barrels harder against Draper's chin. "Because if I don't make it, you sure as hell won't."

"Don't shoot!" Draper shouted with renewed enthusiasm, as if just realizing the truth of Slocum's statement.

"You know what, Draper? It might be safer for both of us if everyone would just throw their guns out into the street," Slocum said.

"Throw your guns out into the street!" Draper ordered.

"What?" someone said. "Damned if I'm going to throw my gun in the street."

"Do it! Just do it!" Draper shouted in a near hysterical voice.

There was a long pause, then one gun came out, then another, and another, until, one by one they began to plop down into the dirt of the street as the little party walked by.

Ian, you keep a good lookout behind us," Slocum said. "I wouldn't want anyone to get brave after we pass them."

"Aye, laddie, I'll keep a sharp eye out," Ian promised.

The train was nearly to the station now and it sounded its whistle again, then it began braking with puffs of steam and the screeching sound of metal on metal. Slocum had come better than fifty yards, just over halfway there.

"Stivers, no!" Draper suddenly shouted. He had spotted one of his men just inside a door, aiming a gun at them. "Put your gun down!"

Stivers hesitated for a moment, then he tossed his gun out.

"Good man, Draper, I see you are watching out for both of us. Now, tell him to come on out into the street."

"Come out!" Draper ordered.

Stivers, with his hands up, came outside to join all the other Crown Ranch riders. By now there were nearly thirty of them and they were all walking quietly down the street behind Slocum and the others, as if this were a giant parade.

In a way, it was a parade, for the rest of the town was watching from their own positions on the sidewalks, and through the windows of their homes and businesses. It was a strange, almost bizarre scene played out in an eerie silence. Slowly, quietly, the parade continued down the street toward the depot.

The conductor was surprised to see that the depot was completely deserted. To the small towns in remote parts of the West, the arrival and departure of trains were the most significant events of the day. Such trains were more than mere conveyances for passengers, or the means of shipping and receiving goods. They were a physical link with the rest of the country, a visible sign that the towns-folk weren't alone. And yet, as the conductor stepped off to give his clarion call, there was not one citizen of Prosperity present to hear him.

"Where is ever . . ." the conductor started, but he stopped when he saw the parade approaching. And at almost the same moment, he saw that the person leading the parade, Seth Draper, had a shotgun jammed up against his chin. "My God! What's going on here?" he asked.

A few of the passengers on the train, who just happened to be looking out the window at what they thought was just one more stop along the way, also saw the strange parade coming toward them. Like the conductor, they were instantly curious, and they left the train to get a better look. Within a few moments, the depot platform was crowded, not with the townspeople who normally gathered to watch the passing of the trains, but with the passengers themselves. It was a strange reversal of normality.

The townspeople weren't left out, though. As the parade had passed them on the street, they left their vantage points and followed. Now, just at the edge of the depot itself, there were nearly three hundred people gathered, representing most of the town and all the passengers on the train.

Just as Slocum arrived at the depot, Caulder stepped out of the crowd and planted himself in the street right in front of Slocum.

"Well, now, you're here," Caulder said, smiling. "I have to tell you, Slocum, I really didn't think you would make it this far. I admire you for that." The smile left his face. "But this is as far as it goes."

"Out of the way, Caulder," Slocum growled.

"Oh? Out of the way or what? You'll kill Draper?"

"You damn right I will."

"Go ahead."

"Caulder!" Draper shouted. "What are you saying? What are you doing? He means it, can't you see that?"

"Oh, yes, I see that. But Slocum knows that I mean it, too. In fact, I understand he played the same game with Mrs. MacTavish. Of course, we don't know if he really meant that or not. Go ahead, Slocum, kill Draper."

"If he's dead, who pays you?" Slocum asked.

"Oh hell, I'm not worried about that," Caulder replied. "I was about ready to move on anyway. But I can't leave without settling the score with you. You understand that, don't you, Slocum? If I let you go, how would that make me look? Why, I'd be the laughingstock of the territory. I'd never get on with anyone else."

"That's probably true," Slocum said. "But that's your problem."

"Not just my problem," Caulder said. "We're going to have to deal with it, both of us, right here, right now. You said it yourself, Slocum. Everyone wants to see us shoot it out." He smiled and took in the crowd with a wave of his hand. "Look how many people are here. Don't you think we owe them a show?"

"Is that really what you want, Caulder?"

"Yeah, that's really what I want. Now, either kill that son of a bitch, or let him go. I really don't care which. Then, let's you and me settle this thing, once and for all."

Slocum eased the hammers down on the shotgun and pulled it away from Draper's chin. He handed the gun to Ian.

"Keep an eye on him," he ordered.

"You've got it," Ian said.

Slocum turned toward Caulder. The crowd backed away to give them more room.

"Ever since you come to town, I've been wonderin' which of us was the fastest," Caulder said.

"Slocum!" Ian shouted, and right on the heels of his shout came a blast from one of the barrels of the shotgun he was holding. Slocum looked up to see Deputy Percy Boyle, his chest and neck blood-splattered from the charge of buckshot, pitching forward off the roof of the private car. Caulder had planted him there as a backup.

When Caulder saw that Boyle was dead and he was going to have to face Slocum alone, the smile on his face faded. Slocum realized then that the advantage had suddenly passed to him. It might have been, all things being equal, that Caulder was as fast, or perhaps even a little faster than Slocum. But Caulder had given himself an edge, and now he saw that edge taken away. That left him with self-doubt, and the self-doubt caused him to feel fear, perhaps for the first time in his life. And that fear was mirrored in his eyes and in the nervous tick on the side of his face. His tongue came out to lick his lips.

Slocum waited, an easy grin spread across his face. Even that, the grin in the face of a life-and-death situation, seemed to unnerve Caulder.

Suddenly Caulder's hand started for his gun, but Slocum's was out just a heartbeat faster. That heartbeat of time was all the advantage Slocum needed, for he fired first. Caulder caught the ball high in his chest. He fired his own gun then, but it was just a convulsive action and the bullet went into the dirt, just before he dropped his gun and slapped his hand over his wound. He looked down in surprise as blood squirted through his fingers, turning his shirt bright red. He took two staggering steps toward Slocum, then fell to his knees. He looked up at Slocum.

"How'd you do that?" he asked in surprise. "How'd you get your gun out that fast?" He smiled, then coughed, and flecks of blood came from his mouth. He breathed hard a couple of times. "I was sure I was faster than you."

"Looks like you were wrong," Slocum said easily.

Caulder fell facedown into the dirt. He was still for a moment, then someone leaned down and put his hand to Caulder's neck. He looked up at the others.

"He's dead," he said.

"Slocum! Look out!" Ian suddenly shouted.

Slocum, who had already returned his pistol to his holster, now spun toward Ian, just in time to see that Draper had somehow managed to get the shotgun away from him.

"I'm going to kill you, you son of a bitch!" Draper shouted, but before he could pull the trigger, even before Slocum could get his own gun out, there was the bang of a gunshot. Slocum saw blood and brain matter explode from the side of Draper's head as he went down, and he turned to his right to see Clint Lane standing there, holding a smoking Colt .44. A flash of sunlight glistened off the sheriff's badge that was pinned to his vest.

Slocum, who had drawn his pistol but hadn't fired, now turned to look at the Crown Ranch riders. Most of them were now unarmed, having thrown their guns into the street during the walk down here.

"It's all over, men," Slocum said. "You've got nobody left to pay your reward. Is there anyone among you who wants to keep this going?"

"I sure as hell don't," a cowboy in the front rank said. "I've had enough of this."

"Me, too," one of the others said.

"Yeah," a third agreed "I'm getting out of here."

One by one the Crown Ranch riders began to walk away. Most of the townspeople returned to their activities as well, though a few of the more morbidly curious hung around a bit longer to look down at the three bodies that had been added to the earlier total.

"All right, folks," the conductor said to the passengers who had been witnesses to the drama. "Let's go. Get back on the train. We've got a schedule to keep."

Slowly, almost reluctantly, the passengers got back onto the train, then it pulled out of the station. Almost as soon as the train left, the switch engine arrived to take the MacTavish car out to Cross Pass Station.

Julie walked over to Slocum and handed him something. When he looked at her questioningly, she said, "It's a bank draft good for fifteen hundred dollars. I believe that was the agreed-upon price?"

"Yes."

"What will you do now?" she asked.

"Move on."

"Where will you go?"

"Nowhere in particular."

"You could stay here, you know. Since Uncle Ian got Crown Ranch returned to him, he has a lot more land to manage than he used to. More land than one man can do alone."

"The offer is tempting."

"I come with the offer, John," Julie said provocatively.

"That makes it even more tempting."

Julie looked at John and read him correctly. The enticing smile on her face was replaced by a look of disappointment, but not anger.

"You are tempted, but you won't come, will you?" she said.

"No."

Leaning into him, she kissed him, letting the tip of her tongue flick across his lips just an instant, then withdrawing it.

"It's too bad, John Slocum," she said as she turned and started toward the private car, which was now connected to the engine. "You will never know what you missed."

"It might be better that way," Slocum said. "If I knew what I was giving up, I might kick myself for the next ten years."

"I hope you do," she said sweetly.

Slocum watched her climb into the car. Then she, Ian, and Emma waved good-bye as the engine started to move. He watched the engine and car move from the side track over to the Cross Station spur line, then begin to gain speed. The engine blew its whistle and smoke poured from the stack as it sped down the track, growing smaller and smaller until it was a distant dot on the horizon.

"Señor Slocum?"

Turning, Slocum saw Juanita standing just behind him. "Yes?"

"Señorita MacTavish is not your woman?"

"No."

"But why? She is beautiful, is she not? And she is also rich."

"Yes, she's all those things."

"Then why is she not your woman?"

"She can never be my woman," Slocum said, "because she wants too much of me. She wants me for the rest of my life, and I'm just not ready to make a commitment to one woman for the rest of my life."

"But, with one woman for one night, you would make such a commitment?"

"Yes."

"I think a woman who would get such a commitment for one night would be very lucky," Juanita said.

There was no mistaking the expression on Juanita's face. It was one of intense sexual desire, and she was making it abundantly clear that she would like to be that woman.

"Do you know where such a woman might be found?"

"Sí, señor," Juanita said. She put out her hand. "Come, I will show you."

Slocum followed her. He had been here this long, he could spend one more night in Prosperity.

Watch for

SLOCUM AND THE LADY IN BLACK

282nd novel in the exciting SLOCUM series
from Jove

Coming in August!